W9-BMV-114

UNLIMITED

KEVIN MILLER

MILLSTONE
PRESS

Copyright © 2017 Kevin Miller

All rights reserved. No part of this publication may be reproduced, distributed, or transmitted in any form or by any means, without prior written permission from the author, except brief excerpts for review purposes.

Kevin Miller/Millstone Press
Box 380
Kimberley, BC, Canada V1A 2Y9

www.millstonepress.ca
www.facebook.com/MilliganCreekSeries

Unlimited/Kevin Miller. -- 1st ed.
ISBN-13: 978-1548244590/10: 1548244597

Cover illustration by Kierston Vande Kraats (https://kvdk.carbonmade.com)

Title design by Huw Miller

Dedication

For Heidi, Huw, Gretchen, Zeph, and Lark, my favorite people in the world.

CONTENTS

1

INTRUDER ALERT!

"And now, the moment you've all been waiting for. We've counted them down, from the bottom to the top, but one song remains. In a surprise turn of events that is sure to rock the entire rock 'n' roll world, this week's number one song on American Top Forty is—"

The DJ's voice exploded in a burst of static, and then the radio went dead.

Dean Muller leaped up from his desk, where he had been listening to the radio while doing his math homework. "Come on, you can't quit on me now!"

At twelve years of age, the freckle-faced boy was an avid American Top Forty listener, so obsessed with tracking the latest pop hits that he kept a detailed logbook noting the weekly ups and downs of his favorite artists, whose posters were plastered across the slanting walls of his attic bedroom.

Dean grabbed his radio and shook it. Nothing. He followed the cord to the wall. It was plugged in. What could possibly be wrong with it?

Just as he was about to open the back of the radio to see if he could to fix it, he heard something from the speaker. He held it to his ear, and a burst of static nearly imploded his eardrum. He jumped back in surprise, bobbled the radio, and then dropped it. He kicked out his foot at the last second and cushioned its fall, nearly doing the splits in the process.

"Ow!"

Just as he was trying to figure out which hurt more, his foot or his ear, a strange electronic tone sounded on his radio, followed by a muffled voice.

"We interrupt this program to bring you an important message. Scientists at the University of Saskatchewan's astronomical observatory have detected a strange atmospheric disturbance over the south-central region of the province. Reports are coming in from numerous communities throughout the area, including descriptions of strange floating lights. Anyone who sees such a phenomenon is asked to contact the local authorities immediately. Whatever you do, do not—I repeat—do not approach the lights. Scientists have yet to determine exactly what they are, but they have not ruled out the possibility of extraterrestrial origin, or some form of sneak attack by the Russians. We now return to your regularly scheduled programming."

His interest in that week's top forty forgotten, Dean winced as he eased himself out of the splits. He turned down the radio and looked out the window. All he saw was his reflection. He switched off his desk lamp and looked out again. Nothing but blackness.

He left his bedroom and crept down the stairs, grimacing each time a board creaked. Before he entered the kitchen, he slid his hand around the corner and turned off the lights. He didn't like the darkness, but if anyone—or anything—was lurking outside, it would make it harder to see him.

He snatched a note off the table and read it in the dim light of the streetlight shining through the window over the kitchen sink. It confirmed that his parents would not be back until around nine o' clock. They had been gone the entire day in Saskatoon for medical appointments and shopping. That meant for the next hour, Dean would be all alone in a dark, empty house with aliens or possibly Russian soldiers lurking outside.

Dean peeked out the window and was blinded by a flash of light. He ducked, his heartbeat slowing only slightly as he watched headlight beams sweep across the kitchen wall. A false alarm. Or was it?

He glanced around for a weapon. He spotted the broom leaning in the corner beside the refrigerator. Too flimsy. His eyes flew to the knife drawer. Too far away. Then he looked at the kitchen island. That's when he spotted it: a meat tenderizer hammer. It was made of wood, but it had a studded metal plate on its face. It would have to do.

Crawling across the floor, Dean reached up and grabbed it off the island, careful to keep out of sight. He clutched the hammer and took a few practice swings. He felt better already. Then he spotted the phone. Of course! His parents were gone, but that didn't mean he had to face down the end of the world on his own.

He crawled over to the phone and was about to lift the beige receiver when it rang. Dean yanked his hand back as if he'd been electrocuted. Who could it be? After a moment's hesitation, he knocked the receiver off its cradle and caught it before it hit the floor. Taking a deep breath, he held it to his ear.

"H-hello?"

"Is this Dennis Muller?"

"N-no, it's his son, Dean."

"Is your father home?"

"No."

"What about your mother?"

"Who is this?"

"That is not your concern. Are you alone in the house?"

Dean glanced around fearfully. "I-I think so."

"What do you mean you think?"

"I mean, I know. Yes, I'm all alone."

"Get out."

"What?"

"Get out. Now. And take nothing with you."

Dean looked down at the meat tenderizer hammer. "Nothing? Why not? I—"

"Just do as I say!"

The line went dead. Dean stared at the receiver in shock. Then he dropped it and the hammer and raced for the front door.

Dean burst outside, ran a few steps, and then dove beneath the lilac bushes that lined the sidewalk, the musty smell of rotting leaves wafting up from the damp ground as he looked back at his house. Nothing seemed out of the ordinary. It just stood there, dark and foreboding. Why had the man on the phone told him to leave?

Dean was so caught up in examining his house that he didn't realize the area around him was growing brighter. It was a reflection off the second-story windows that first caught his attention. Then he glanced down at the damp grass and saw yellow lights dancing over the dewdrops. Not wanting to look up, but not wanting to be taken out unawares, Dean craned his head toward the sky. That's when he saw them: strange floating lights, just like the man on the radio had warned!

Dean flattened himself against the ground, frozen in fear. He couldn't go back inside, and now the aliens or Russians or whatever they were, were outside. What could he do? Unable to handle the tension any longer, he did whatever any other sensible twelve-year-old boy would do in such a situation. He leapt up and ran down the street, screaming like a maniac.

"Help!"

That's when he heard it: laughter.

He slowed and then stopped, looking around in confusion. Couldn't the aliens or Russians just get it over with? Did they have to mock him before they incinerated him? Then he realized the laughter didn't sound like Russians or aliens. In fact, it sounded just like . . .

"Matt Taylor!" Dean exclaimed.

Sporting his trademark Edmonton Oilers cap, Dean's friend, Matt Taylor, his older brother, Chad, and the fourth member of their tight-knit group, Andrew Loewen, emerged from some nearby bushes, all three of them doubled over with laughter.

Dean looked up at the sky and realized the "strange" floating lights weren't so strange after all. They were hot-air balloons made from dry-cleaning bags, which the boys had learned to make at camp the previous summer.

He turned back to his friends, who were beginning to recover from their laughing fit. "Very funny, guys, very funny," he said. Then he frowned. "Wait a second, that was you on the radio?"

Matt choked back his laughter long enough to respond. "Yup."

"And the phone?"

Chad held up his hand. "Guilty."

"How the heck did you do that?"

Still laughing, Matt and Chad pointed at Andrew. "Ask him!" they said in unison.

Andrew held up a black briefcase. Dean stared at it in wonder. "What is it?"

Andrew smiled. "Say hello to . . . the Hijacker."

2

THE HIJACKER

Minutes later, the boys were gathered around Dean's kitchen table, the briefcase at the center.

"What are you waiting for?" Dean asked. "Open it!"

Andrew ceremoniously undid the clasps and then opened the briefcase. The other three boys edged in for a better look as Andrew gave them a guided tour of its contents. It looked like something out of an old spy movie—a tangled mass of wires soldered to a series of circuit boards with glowing lights, all of it powered by a large six-volt battery. Each part of the device was nestled into a hollowed-out area of the briefcase's foam interior.

"I call it the Hijacker," Andrew said, "but it's actually a broadcast signal intruder."

Dean glanced up at his friend, his eyebrows furrowed in confusion. "A what?"

"An FM radio transmitter that can overpower or hijack the same frequency another radio station is using to broadcast. Then, using this microphone here," he pulled it out of the case, "I can broadcast my own message."

"Which is how we made the fake UFO public service announcement," Matt added. "Straight out of 'War of the Worlds.'"

Dean frowned. "War of the what?"

"You know, the famous Halloween radio drama that people thought was a newscast about a real UFO invasion?"

Dean continued to stare at Matt, perplexed.

Matt sighed in exasperation. "Haven't you ever played Trivial Pursuit?"

"Yes, but—"

"Anyway," Andrew continued, "it doesn't have a lot of power, so it has a pretty short range, about twenty-five feet or so. We had to get pretty close to your house to make it work. And apparently, it did."

Dean nodded as he stared at the device, the puzzle pieces finally beginning to assemble in his mind. Then he looked at the telephone hanging on the kitchen wall.

"What about the phone call? Can you hack into phone lines with this thing too?"

"That was me," Chad said. "I called you from the pay phone inside the rink."

Dean shook his head. "Pretty amazing. Except for the fact that now I'll have to wait until next week to see who came in first on American Top Forty, thanks to you three." Then he glanced at the clock. "Hey, I have an idea. My parents should be home in about twenty minutes. Want to use it to play a trick on them?"

Matt's eyes lit up. "That's a great idea! What do you think, Andrew?"

Andrew looked at Dean. "What sort of trick did you have in mind?"

Dean was already running up the stairs to his bedroom. "I'll tell you in a minute. Just let me get my radio!"

Twenty minutes later, the kitchen was empty and silent, except for Dean's radio, which was sitting in the center of the kitchen table playing Corey Hart's "I Wear My

Sunglasses at Night." A moment later, the door opened, and Mrs. Muller burst in, her arms laden with packages from a day of shopping in the city.

"Dean? We're home!" She set the packages on the table and looked around. "Dean?"

Mr. Muller came in behind her, also burdened with bags of groceries. "Where do you want all of this?"

"Just set it on the floor," Mrs. Muller said as she went through the house turning on lights. "Dean?"

She jogged up the stairs, peeked into his bedroom, and flicked on the light. His homework was sitting where he had left it on his desk, but there was no sign of her son. She frowned, a spark of worry igniting in her stomach. "Dennis? Did Dean tell you he was going anywhere tonight?"

When she entered the kitchen, she found her husband staring at Dean's radio, frowning.

"Dennis, what—"

He held up a hand to silence her, then pointed at the radio, which was broadcasting a man's voice. ". . . scientists are calling the turn of events unprecedented, a disease that only affects children and young teens. To prevent it from spreading to the general population, all children under fifteen years of age have been rounded up and taken into government facilities, where they will be quarantined until further notice. We now return you to your regular programming." As if on cue, the radio cut to "Don't You Forget About Me" by Simple Minds.

Mrs. Muller stared at her husband in shock. "I can't believe it. My baby—quarantined!"

Mr. Muller sighed, familiar with his wife's frequent emotional outbursts. "Now let's not get too carried away, Audrey. Just because some children have been rounded up doesn't mean Dean has. They're probably just talking about major population centers."

"Then where is he?" Mrs. Muller demanded, putting her hands on her hips.

"Over at a friend's house, perhaps?" Mr. Muller suggested patiently.

His wife shook her head, her eyes already glassy with tears. "No, I can feel it in my heart." She put her hand to her chest. "My baby, my Deanie Zucchini, is in exile. A hostage, a prisoner, taken by his own government!"

As she broke down in tears, Mr. Muller embraced her, at a loss for how to respond. He had a hard time believing his son had been rounded up and placed in quarantine. At the same time, he couldn't come up with a reasonable explanation for Dean's absence. Even if Dean had gone over to a friend's house, he certainly would have left a note.

As those thoughts ran through his mind, he heard something that didn't come from the radio or his sobbing wife.

A giggle.

His eyes flew to the broom closet. He released his wife, which only caused her to clutch onto him even harder.

"Just a minute, Audrey," he said, prying her fingers off his arm. "I think I may have just solved this mystery."

He whipped open the broom closet door, revealing Dean, Matt, Chad, and Andrew stuffed inside. Matt held up his hand and waved. "Good evening, Mr. Muller!"

At the sound of Matt's voice, Mrs. Muller's head whipped around, and her tear-stained face exploded in shock, and then anger. "Matt Taylor? What on earth are you doing in my house—and in my broom closet?"

Matt grinned as he held up a pink feather duster and pretended to dust Dean's face. "Oh, you know, just helping 'Deanie Zucchini' here with the housew—"

His words were choked off as Dean elbowed him in the ribs and then forced his way out of the closet. "Sorry, Mom. We were just hiding to play a trick on you."

Mrs. Muller wiped her face, already recovering from her fright now that Dean was standing in front of her. "Well, I don't think it's very funny. And who gave you permission to have friends over? You're supposed to be doing your homework. But forget about that. I want you to sit right down in this chair so I can look you over. Dennis, get the thermometer."

Mr. Muller looked at her. "What for?"

"So I can see if he's sick. You heard what the man said on the radio."

Dean held up his hands in protest. "But Mom, it wasn't real. I'm not—" He cowered at the sight of his mother's pointing finger.

"I've already heard enough out of you, young man. As for the rest of you," she turned to Matt, Chad, and Andrew as they spilled out of the broom closet like clowns emerging from a tiny car, "you would do well to go home and have your mothers examine you. And don't blame me if you get rounded up like stray dogs along the way."

"But Mom, it wasn't—"

"Yes, Mrs. Muller," Matt said, motioning for Dean to keep quiet as he and the other boys headed toward the door.

"We're sorry we frightened you," Chad said on his way out.

"It would have been funny—if not for that broadcast," Mr. Muller said.

"No, it wouldn't have!" Mrs. Muller cried. Her eyes shot down to the briefcase Andrew was carrying. "What are you supposed to be, some kind of traveling salesman?"

Andrew glanced down at the case. "Yeah, uh, something like that."

"Well, whatever it is, we're not buying. As for you, Dean Muller, what did I say the punishment was for having friends over without permission—and on a school night, no less?"

Dean sighed. "Grounding."

"Exactly." Mrs. Muller folded her arms across her chest. "I hope you boys are satisfied with yourselves. Apart from classes and other mandatory events, you won't be seeing Dean for a week."

Mr. Muller held the door open for Matt, Chad, and Andrew. "She'll cool down once she gets over her shock," he whispered.

"I heard that!" Mrs. Muller said. "And no, I won't!"

As the door closed behind his friends, Dean slumped even further into his chair.

Mrs. Muller scowled at her husband. "Don't just stand there. Get me the thermometer!"

3

HENRIETTA BLUNT

Air brakes hissed as a big yellow school bus slowed down and turned past a sign that read, "Welcome to the Milligan Creek Heritage Marsh."

On board in the front seat was Mrs. Tammy Kowalski, who taught junior high science at Milligan Creek Composite School. A veteran teacher, her many years of service had done nothing to dampen her enthusiasm. She stood up and faced the back of the bus, which was packed with chattering students from grades seven to nine. It smelled vaguely of banana skins moldering in abandoned brown paper lunch bags.

"Okay, students, listen up." She paused until the conversations died down completely. "I want you all on your best behavior today. No fooling around, and no wandering off on your own. Ms. Blunt and Wetlands Unlimited have been kind enough to host us for the day and to give us a guided tour of the marsh, so let's make sure we show our appreciation by being on our best behavior. Understood?"

"Yes, Mrs. Kowalski," the students chorused.

"And just to make sure you do pay attention, we'll be doing a quiz tomorrow on some of the things we learn today, so listen up!"

Her announcement was met with a series of groans as the students stood up and gathered their things.

"This is the best day ever!" Matt exclaimed as he grabbed his backpack from under the seat in front of him. "Field trip!"

"It's not exactly Disneyland," Chad remarked, gesturing to the acres of bulrushes that surrounded the marsh's broad, watery expanse, which glinted in the warm morning sunlight.

"Yeah, but it's a day off school. What could be better than that?"

"I'll tell you what could be better: you being grounded for a change instead of me."

The boys turned toward Dean, who remained in his seat with his backpack in his lap.

"Look on the bright side, Dean," Chad said. "At least we're not stuck in the classroom."

"No, but I've been stuck on this bus for the past forty-five minutes, and now I'm carsick."

Matt smirked. "Don't you mean 'bus sick'?"

Chad frowned at his younger brother and then pushed past him and held out his hand to Dean. "Come on, the fresh air'll do you good."

Dean let out a huge sigh. Then he locked wrists with Chad and allowed him to pull him to his feet. Both boys followed the other students off the bus.

The moment he stepped outside, Dean covered his nose and mouth with his hand and gagged. "Aaaghh, what's that smell?"

"Yeah," Matt agreed, holding his nose. "I thought we were touring a duck marsh, not a sewage treatment plant."

"Ah, my young feathered friends, but this is a sewage treatment plant—a waterfowl sewage treatment plant."

The four boys and the rest of the students fell silent as

they turned toward the voice. Their eyes were met by a tall, gangly woman dressed in a khaki uniform with matching ball cap, both of which were emblazoned with the Wetlands Unlimited logo, and a black fanny pack around her waist. She closed her eyes, held out her arms, took a huge breath through her nose, held it for a moment, and then let it out slowly through her mouth. Then she opened her eyes and smiled at the stunned students, her blue eyes sparkling with excitement.

"Isn't it wonderful? Millions—billions—of microbes hard at work twenty-four hours a day, seven days a week, breaking down plant and animal matter in an anaerobic environment and pumping methane, hydrogen sulfide, and carbon dioxide into the atmosphere. And all you need to do to appreciate the fruit of their labor of love is the one thing that comes naturally to every human being on this planet: breathe. Altogether now. In . . ." She closed her eyes and took another huge breath. ". . . and out." She let out the breath through pursed lips, her eyes still closed, completely unaware of the seventy students staring at her in disbelief, not one of them following her example.

"Ah, you must be Ms. Blunt," Mrs. Kowalski said, stepping forward and cringing slightly as she held out her hand. "I'm Tammy Kowalski."

Henrietta opened her eyes and smiled. "Pleased to meet you, Tammy. Call me Henrietta." She shook her hand vigorously. "Henrietta Blunt, that is, wetlands and waterfowl expert at your service."

She released Mrs. Kowalski's hand and turned to the students. "This is going to be a fantastic day! Now, if you'll all follow me, I'll review the health and safety guidelines with you before we proceed to our brand-new boardwalk for a tour of the marsh. And keep your eyes and ears peeled! This morning, I heard a red-breasted merganser.

I haven't seen him yet, but the first person who does gets a prize!"

As Henrietta headed toward a big wooden sign that outlined the marsh's code of conduct, Mrs. Kowalski and the other students trailing behind her, Matt stood in place and shook his head in disbelief. "You were wrong, Chad."

Chad stopped and looked at his brother. "What do you mean?"

"This *is* Disneyland, and she's Daffy."

"Uh, Daffy's a Looney Tunes character," Andrew replied. "If this is Disneyland, she's Donald."

Chad looked at him. "Don't you mean Daisy? Ms. Blunt is a woman, remember?"

"Whatever her name is," Dean said, pushing past them, "she's definitely a quack."

The other boys laughed as they hurried to catch up with the group.

§

Thirty minutes later, the students were standing on the boardwalk that zigzagged through the marsh, their eyes glazed over as Henrietta continued her lecture on the importance of the province's wetlands.

"This marsh may seem like nothing more than a stinky slough, but it's actually a lush oasis in the middle of the prairies that performs all sorts of important ecological functions. In addition to providing a home for several species of waterfowl, muskrats, beavers, and many other forms of life, it cleans the water that runs off the surrounding fields and helps protect the local area from flooding and drought. Now, this place is called a marsh, but who can tell me the difference between a marsh, a bog, a fen, and a swamp?"

Her question was met by dead silence and blank faces, but that only deepened her enthusiasm. "Come on now," she said with a huge grin, "don't be shy. To live is to learn."

Mrs. Kowalski frowned at the students. "If you don't know, at least take a guess."

Andrew looked around at the other students and then slowly raised his hand. Henrietta pointed to him. "Yes, you in the back."

Andrew cleared his throat. "I could be wrong, but if I remember correctly, a swamp is a wetland where the plants are primarily trees; a marsh has no trees, just reeds and grass; a bog is characterized by poor soil with a high peat content; and a fen is like a bog but with more plant life and less peat."

Everyone—including Henrietta—stared at Andrew in awestruck silence. Then she pushed through the crowd until she was standing face to face with him. She put her hands on her hips and shook her head slowly from side to side. "Unbelievable."

Andrew looked around at the other students uncertainly. "I'm sorry, I just—"

"In all my years leading tours in wetlands across this province, I have never heard such a succinct, well-informed explanation, and from such a handsome young man too!"

Andrew's face flushed in embarrassment.

"That, my friend, deserves a prize, and I have just the thing." She dug into her fanny pack, pulled something out, and held it up for all to see. "Your very own Wetlands Unlimited sticker!"

When no one reacted, she frowned at the students. "Come on, now."

The students looked around hesitantly, and then someone started to clap. Soon, others followed suit.

"That's more like it!"

Henrietta peeled the back off the sticker and then thumped it onto Andrew's chest. "Wear it proudly, young man." She leaned in close and winked. "I don't hand those out to just anyone!"

Then she stepped back and held up her hand as if she wanted him to high five her. Andrew looked around uncertainly, blushing an even deeper shade of red as the other students giggled.

Henrietta grinned. "Come on now, don't leave me hanging."

Finally, Andrew high fived her.

"Yes! Learning is awesome!" She brought her fist down hard like a hockey player who had just scored a goal and then turned back to the group. "Alright, people, let's keep moving. There's so much more to see and do!"

As she started down the boardwalk, Matt nudged Andrew. "Andy's got a girlfriend."

Andrew shoved him. "Shut up!"

Matt stumbled backward toward the boardwalk railing, but Chad caught him. After helping Matt regain his balance, Chad leaned over the railing and looked down at the dark water. "Wonder how deep it is."

"Probably only a foot or two," Andrew said, coming up beside him, "but the mud beneath it? Your guess is as good as mine."

"One way to find out." Matt grabbed a stick that was floating beside the boardwalk and shoved it into the water. He hit mud almost immediately and kept pushing it down until the stick and his hand disappeared beneath the water. When he pulled it out, three feet of the four-foot stick was dripping with smelly, black mud.

"Yuck!" Dean exclaimed.

Matt held it closer to him. "Come on, Dean, you heard

what Henrietta said. Breathe . . . in . . . and out."

"Get that thing away from me!" He gave Matt a shove.

"Boys! What are you doing?"

All four of them turned to see Mrs. Kowalski glaring at them. Matt dropped the stick on the boardwalk, spattering Dean's pants with mud.

Dean looked down and scowled. "Hey!"

Oblivious, Matt smiled and wiped his hand on his jacket. "Sorry, Mrs. Kowalski. Andrew was just instructing us a bit more on the ratio of peat to mud in a typical marsh."

Her face softened. "Well, that's very clever of him, but right now, we're here to learn from Ms. Blunt. Now get a move on."

"Yes, Mrs. Kowalski," the boys replied.

When they caught up to the group, they had just reached the top of a three-story wooden observation tower that overlooked a wide expanse of open water. Henrietta was pointing to a muskrat house, a small mound of reeds and mud sticking out of the water.

"Anyone want to guess how long a muskrat can hold its breath?"

A student held up his hand. "Two minutes?"

Henrietta smiled and shook her head. "Higher."

"Five?" someone else suggested.

"Higher!"

"Ten?"

"Higher!"

"Fifteen?"

"Close enough! A typical muskrat can stay underwater for twelve to seventeen minutes. Imagine that! Like whales, their bodies are not as sensitive to the buildup of carbon dioxide in the bloodstream as other mammals. Not only that, they have an extra layer of fur to keep them warm in the cold water, webbed feet, and they can close their ears to keep the water out. Isn't that amazing? They're like a prairie submarine! Okay, before we proceed to the interpretive center, any questions?"

She held her hand over her eyes to shield them from the sun reflecting off the water as she scanned the group.

A boy with a classic case of bedhead put up his hand. "Are there any cows in the swamp?"

Henrietta looked a bit confused by the question. "It's a marsh, not a swamp, as you'll recall, and no, there are no cows here. Why do you ask?"

The boy smiled. "I like cows."

Henrietta chuckled. "What's your name, young man?"

"Ben."

"Well, I like cows too, Ben—especially on my dinner plate! But agricultural run-off is considered one of today's biggest environmental threats, polluting bodies of water with bovine fecal matter, a.k.a. manure, something we're constantly trying to educate farmers about. Any other questions?"

A moment later, Matt put up his hand.

"Yes?" Henrietta said.

Matt pointed out over the water. "What's that?"

Everyone turned to see what he was looking at.

"That, my friend, is the interpretive center. That's where we're headed next. It's full of all sorts of displays, and—"

"I'm sorry, I meant that tall thing standing next to it," he said, pointing to a seventy-five-foot-tall radio tower attached to the building.

Mrs. Kowalski frowned at Matt for interrupting Henrietta, but the chipper guide just smiled and turned back to the group. "That is a surprise I was going to save until the end of our tour, but I suppose now is as good a time as any."

She dug into her fanny pack and pulled out a small transistor radio. She held it up and turned it on. After a brief burst of static, a voice came on. ". . . to the Milligan Creek Heritage Marsh, where you'll find up to sixty pairs of breeding waterfowl per square mile, including sandhill cranes, garganeys, red-winged blackbirds, black-bellied plovers, snow geese, Canada geese and, of course, ducks!"

She lowered the radio and turned down the volume. "Anyone notice something familiar about that voice?"

At first, no one answered. Then Mrs. Kowalski raised her hand. "Is that you?"

Henrietta beamed. "That's right! Broadcasting around the clock, it's our new Wetlands Unlimited radio station! Night or day, you can tune in to hear the latest wetlands news, which I'll be recording weekly, announcing new migrations, special tours, rare sightings, and all sorts of other interesting events. Okay, now that the cat's out of the bag, we can—" She paused when she saw Matt's hand shoot up again. "Yes?"

"How far does your radio station reach? I mean, can we listen to it at school?"

"Excellent question! Yes, thanks to a generous government grant and several private donations, we have installed a powerful FM transmitter that reaches up to thirty-five kilometers in all directions. So, whether you're at home or at school, night or day, tune in to ninety-eight point seven on your FM dial, and you'll be able to hear me warble about the wetlands!"

Matt smiled. "Awesome!"

Henrietta looked around. "Any more questions? No? Okay, we'll move on."

As the other students followed Henrietta, Matt remained in place, his eyes fixed on the radio tower.

"Uh oh," Chad said, coming alongside his brother. "Matt's wheels are turning."

"I thought I smelled wood burning," Dean quipped.

Chad and Andrew laughed, but Matt didn't respond to the gibe, as he normally would.

"What's on your mind, bro?" Chad asked.

Matt glanced at Andrew. "That hijacker thing you made, you still have it, right?"

"Yeah, why?"

Matt turned back to the tower and grinned. "I think I just came up with a whole new use for it."

4

THE TEST

"You can't be serious," Dean said. "It's got to be illegal."

The boys were gathered in their "headquarters," a tree house in the dense shelter belt of poplar and aspen trees that surrounded the Taylors' yard. The structure consisted, in part, of a vintage MD 500 Defender helicopter fuselage, complete with a round bubble windshield. The helicopter had crashed and burned, but Matt and Chad's father, who was a spray plane pilot, had picked it up cheap at a salvage auction. Then he and the boys renovated it for their purposes, installing new glass and four bucket seats as well as electricity, which they ran from the yard light.

The rest of the tree house was more traditional, made from a hodgepodge of salvaged wood, old windows, and a metal roof. It was an ongoing construction project, with the boys constantly adding new features, including bunk beds, bookshelves, a mini fridge, shutters, and window boxes full of flowers, which were Dean's pet project. The other boys teased him about his green thumb, but they had to admit the flowers gave the tree house a homey touch, not to mention a pleasant smell when the windows were open.

Dean was leaning out the window watering the flowers. His mother had lifted his grounding early in an uncharacteristic act of mercy, thanks in no small part to Dean volunteering to do a heap of extra chores.

"I think 'illegal' is stretching things a bit," Matt said. "All we'd be doing is borrowing or hitchhiking."

"Or hijacking," Dean said. "Which is a crime in pretty much every country." He glanced up from his flowers and saw the other three boys staring at him. "Don't look at me," he said. "I didn't name the device." He pointed his watering can at Andrew. "He did."

"He has a point," Andrew admitted, looking down at the black briefcase, which lay open on the table in front of him, its complicated electronics exposed.

"So, we change the name," Matt said. "It's not like we're using guns and taking hostages. Call it the hitchhiker then. Hitchhiking's not illegal."

"It is in some places," Chad pointed out.

"And it's customary to ask permission before entering someone's vehicle, is it not?" Dean asked.

"My point," Matt said, beginning to pace, "is that to have a crime, you need a victim, and I don't see how anyone could possibly be victimized by what I'm proposing. We do it in the middle of the night when nobody's listening, just one time, and just to see if it works." He looked at Andrew and smiled, hoping to appeal to his scientific curiosity. "Think of it as an experiment."

"Why don't we just ask permission?" Chad said.

Matt looked at his brother. "Are you kidding me? You met Ms. Blunt. There's no way she'll agree. All wetlands, all the time, that's her motto."

"I am kind of curious to see if I can make it work," Andrew admitted, adjusting a few wires on the device. "It's one thing to override a signal at the receiving end, but doing it at the transmitter is another thing altogether. I think I can figure it out though. And I agree with Matt. If we just do it once, I don't see what—or who—it would harm."

"We'd have to trespass," Dean said. "That's definitely against the law."

"Not necessarily," Andrew remarked, leaning back in his bucket seat and staring at the ceiling, a thoughtful look on his face.

Matt plopped down in the seat beside him and pushed back his Edmonton Oilers cap. "What do you have in mind?"

Andrew was quiet for a moment. Then he leaned forward and looked at the other boys. "Think you guys can sneak out and meet at around midnight this Friday?"

Matt grinned at Chad, who nodded, and then turned back to Andrew. "Of course!"

The other boys all looked at Dean. He held up his hands in self-defense. "Forget it! I just got un-grounded, remember?" The boys continued to stare at him. Finally, he slammed the watering can down in disgust. "Oh, all right, but just this once!"

Matt smiled and rubbed his hands together in anticipation. "Excellent. Andrew, just tell us what we need to do to get ready."

§

Shortly after midnight that Friday, four black-clad figures raced down a gravel road on their bicycles. Two of them, Andrew and Chad, also wore backpacks. When they reached the entry to the marsh, they concealed their bikes in the ditch and then crept across a neighboring field to the edge of the water. The only sounds they heard were a slight breeze and the murmuring of birds bedded down in the bulrushes for the night.

Andrew and Chad opened their packs. Andrew pulled

out the Hijacker, a foam flutter board, some rope, a roll of duct tape, and a plastic garbage bag. He opened the Hijacker and turned it on. Then he closed it and wrapped it in the garbage bag, sealing it with the duct tape. He used the tape to attach it to the flutter board. When he was done, he set it in the water and then tested it to make sure it wouldn't capsize.

Satisfied, he returned to the group, where Chad was setting up their other vital piece of equipment: a remote-controlled speedboat Andrew had gotten for Christmas a couple of years earlier. They tied some fishing line from the boat to the flutter board and then set the boat in the water.

Chad handed the remote control to Andrew. "You drive," he whispered. "I don't want to be responsible if it sinks."

Dean looked around nervously. "Shh . . .."

Matt grinned. "What, are you worried the cows will hear us?"

As if in response, a cow mooed quietly in the distance. Chad giggled.

"Quiet!" Dean whispered.

"Do you have the mic?" Andrew asked.

Matt turned on a wireless microphone. "Got it."

"Radio?"

"Right here." Dean held it up.

"Turn it on," Andrew said.

Dean did, and suddenly Henrietta Blunt's voice blared across the previously silent marsh. They all hit the dirt as Dean scrambled to turn down the volume. "Sorry!" he whispered. "I thought I had checked that earlier."

They waited for a moment, but they didn't hear or see anything unusual, so they resumed their preparations.

"I wish we could have done a mic test beforehand,"

Andrew said. "I'm not even sure this thing'll reach that far. If it doesn't work, we won't know if it's the device or the mic."

"Don't worry about it," Matt said. "If it doesn't work, I'll just get closer."

"You'll be trespassing," Dean warned.

"Yes, and all in the name of science," Matt replied.

"Okay, let's do this," Chad said, sweeping his hair out of his eyes as he checked his watch. "I want to get back home before Mom and Dad realize we're gone."

Andrew pushed the throttle forward, and the boat set out across the marsh.

"Bon voyage!" Matt whispered.

The boat's tiny electric motor whined as it pulled the Hijacker across the water.

"I'm worried the motor's going to burn out," Andrew said. "I hope it's not pulling too much weight."

"Just take it slow," Chad replied, shining a flashlight on the boat, so Andrew could track its progress, aided in part by the gibbous moon.

As the boat neared the interpretive center, Andrew turned to Matt. "Okay, try it now."

Matt held the microphone to his mouth as Dean held the radio to his ear. "Testing, one, two, three. Testing . . ." He looked at Dean, who shook his head.

"Nothing."

"You have to get it closer, Andy," Matt said.

"I'm worried about it getting snagged in the bulrushes," Andrew replied, straining to see the boat, which was nearly beyond the reach of Chad's flashlight.

Chad glanced back at his brother. "Try it again."

"Testing, one, two, three. Testing—"

"I can hear you!" Dean shouted.

"Shhh . . ." the other three boys whispered.

In response, Dean turned up the radio, which was still broadcasting Henrietta's voice. "Do it again."

"Testing, one, two, three . . ." This time, Matt's voice came through loud and clear on the radio. "It works!" he cried. Then he held the microphone back to his lips. "This is your commander speaking," his voice boomed. As he continued to talk, Dean tried to turn down the volume. "Resistance is futile. Milligan Creek is surrounded. Surrender or die. You have twenty seconds to comply."

When the others shushed him, Matt waved them off and put his arm around Andrew's shoulders. "Andrew, my friend, you're a genius!"

Andrew smiled bashfully as Dean turned off the radio. "Thank God that's over," Dean said. "Let's get out of here before we get into trouble.

"For once, I agree with you," Matt replied, glancing around. "We can't have anyone getting grounded if we hope to pull off phase two."

Dean's forehead furrowed in confusion. "Phase two? Who said anything about phase two?"

Chad smiled. "Dean, when it comes to Matt, you should know there's always a phase two."

5

It Came . . . from the Grain!

"We have the power," Matt said as he chewed his baloney and mustard sandwich at noon hour the next day, "but what are we going to do with it?"

"Keep it down," Dean said, glancing furtively at the crowded lunchroom. Thankfully, none of the other students seemed to be paying attention. "You don't want to blow our cover."

Matt chuckled. "Relax, Dean. No one has any idea what we're talking about."

"It is a pretty incredible opportunity," Andrew said.

Chad looked at him and smiled. "Andy, I didn't realize you were such a rebel!"

"That's where all great scientific discoveries are made," Andrew replied. "On the edge of what's acceptable—or allowed."

Matt smacked the table. "So that's what I've been all along. A scientist!"

Other students looked at him. He smiled and gave a small wave.

"Ha!" Dean scoffed. "You got a sixty-five in math—and that was with me helping you."

Matt waved him off. "A minor detail."

"What about if we start off by broadcasting some music?" Chad suggested.

"Yeah, rock 'n' roll," Matt replied.

"What about classical?" Andrew said.

Matt nodded. "Yeah, classic rock."

"No, I meant classical, with flutes and strings and stuff, like on CBC radio."

Matt tilted his head back in disgust. "Boorring . . .."

"Jazz?" Chad offered.

Matt looked at his brother. "Are you guys nuts?"

Dean held up his index finger. "How about—"

"No, we're not doing American Top Forty," Matt said without even bothering to look at him. "There's no way I could DJ any of that stuff."

Dean frowned. "Who says you're the DJ?"

"I just assumed—"

"Maybe music's not such a good idea," Chad said, seeking to head off another argument. "Besides, everyone broadcasts music. If we're going to start our own radio station, we should at least do something original."

Matt nodded. "Good point."

The boys fell silent, deep in thought as they chewed their sandwiches. Suddenly, Matt's eyes lit up. "I've got it!"

He was about to share his idea when the bell rang, ending lunch hour. "I'll tell you about it later," he said, standing up. "Dean's right; too many listening ears around here. Let's meet at the tree house after school."

§

Three hours later, Matt and Andrew were sitting in their bucket seats inside the helicopter fuselage. Chad grabbed some cans of pop from their mini fridge. Just as he was about to set them on the table, the trapdoor popped open, and Dean climbed up, huffing with exertion. "Sorry I'm late, guys. Paper route."

"You're just in time," Chad said, tossing Dean a can of pop. Dean bobbled it and dropped it.

"Fire in the hole!" Andrew cried.

"Here, better open this one instead," Chad said. He handed Dean another can and then put the first one back into the fridge.

"Thanks." Dean plunked down in his seat. "Man, it's hot out there." He opened his can of pop and took a long drink, downing nearly half of it in one gulp.

"So, what's the big idea, little brother?" Chad said, sitting down and swiveling toward Matt.

Matt grinned. "You're going to love this."

"I doubt that," Dean said, slurping up the leftover pop from the rim of his can.

"Five words," Matt continued, undaunted. "It Came . . . from the Grain."

Dean gave Matt a skeptical look. "What?"

"It Came . . . from the Grain," Matt repeated ominously.

Chad held up his hands in confusion. "I'm with Dean. What the heck are you talking about?"

"I think I know," Andrew said. "You're talking about a radio play. Like 'War of the Worlds.'"

Matt pointed at him and grinned. "Exactly!"

"I don't know." Dean swiped condensation from the side of his pop can and then licked his finger. "Hasn't it already been done?"

"Of course, it's been done," Matt replied. "That's all people listened to before TV came along. But it's never been done like this."

Chad leaned forward in his chair. "So, 'It Came from the Grain,' that's the title?"

Matt nodded. "Yes."

"What's it about?" Andrew asked.

"I don't know. That's what I was hoping you guys could help me figure out. But I think it should be something scary, suspenseful, with each episode ending on a cliff-hanger."

Dean raised his eyebrows. "Each episode? You mean we're going to do this more than once?"

"Of course!" Matt replied. "It's too much work coming up with an idea to do it just once."

"So, let me get this straight," Chad said, thinking out loud, "you want us to stand on the edge of the marsh performing a radio play in the middle of the night?"

"Yes!"

"Well, you can count me out." Dean got up to check on his flowers. "Too risky."

"I have a better idea," Andrew said, steepling his fingers in front of his face. He waited until he had everyone's full attention before continuing. "We record it beforehand and then hook up a tape player to the Hijacker, along with a timer."

Chad's eyes lit up. "Could you do that?"

"With a few modifications."

"But that still means sneaking out late at night once a week," Dean objected. "It's only a matter of time until we get caught."

"Not necessarily," Andrew said. "We can sneak the tape into the Hijacker during the day and then set the timer so that it begins broadcasting at midnight."

"That's brilliant!" Matt exclaimed. "I love it!"

"I do too," Chad replied. "But we still don't know what 'It Came from the Grain' is about."

"Well, think about it." Matt sat back in his chair and looked out the window. "Who or what might be hidden in a grain field?"

The other boys also leaned back in their chairs, deep in thought.

"A shotgun?" Chad suggested a moment later.

"Too violent," Matt said. "You'd have to see it go off at some point. How about a dead body?"

Chad looked at him. "And that's not violent?"

"Not if it's already dead."

"What if dead people rise from the field whenever it rains?" Andrew asked. "You know, like zombies?"

"More dead bodies?" Dean shook his head. "Uh-uh."

"Besides, zombies have been done to death," Matt said. "Get it?"

The other boys groaned at his lame pun.

"Maybe the field whispers romantic advice to someone whenever the wind blows from a certain direction," Chad said. "You know, like that movie with Steve Martin about the guy with the big nose who helps the young guy win the girl."

"Roxanne," Andrew said.

Chad nodded. "That's the one. And maybe the field is owned by his romantic rival, and he realizes what's going on, so he sets out to combine it before it can deliver the last piece of advice that will seal the deal."

"A romance?" Matt said. "Come on."

"It could be a romantic comedy."

Matt grimaced at his brother. "Even worse. This is supposed to be scary, remember? 'It Came . . . from the Grain'!" he said in a menacing tone.

"I know what could come out of the field," Dean said, leaning forward. "A ball."

The other boys looked at him. "A ball?" Matt said. "That's not scary."

"It could be," Dean replied. "Think about it. You're walking along the edge of this huge grain field right before harvest. It's tall and golden and waving in the wind. Suddenly, out of the field bounces a rubber ball, one that's half red and half blue with a white line around the middle. You pick it up and look at it. Then you throw it back into the grain field as hard as you can."

"Why would you throw away a perfectly good ball?" Matt asked.

"I'm not finished," Dean said. "You throw the ball, and you keep walking, and suddenly, the ball comes bouncing out of the field again. Weird, right?"

Matt shrugged. "I guess so."

"So, you throw it in a completely different direction, and once again, moments later, it comes flying back at you."

"That is kind of creepy," Chad admitted.

Andrew looked at Dean. "Who's throwing the ball back at you?"

Dean paused to think. "I don't know . . . little people."

Matt frowned. "Little people?"

"Yeah. They hatch every year the grain is planted, and then they disappear at harvest."

Andrew nodded thoughtfully. "Okay, so, how's the ball fit in?"

Dean tapped his finger on his chin as he thought about it. "Maybe the little people can't leave the grain field, but they see a kid walking along and think he's a little person, just like them, so they want to lure him into the field to see what makes him different. They think if they're able to leave the grain field, they'll be able to live longer than just one season. But once they realize the kid is just that, a kid, they decide to hold him hostage instead. Then they try to lure other kids into the field in the hope that they can stop the farmer from harvesting it, and they won't disappear."

"Not bad," Chad said. "Did you just come up with that right now?"

40

Dean downed the last of his pop and then wiped his mouth with the back of his hand. "Yeah."

"You should write it as a short story," Matt said, "but I don't think it works as a radio play."

Dean looked at him. "Why not?"

"Because little people aren't scary. Besides, whoever played the little people would have to suck on helium each time they delivered a line of dialogue."

The boys became quiet once again, deep in thought. As they pondered ideas, a leaf blew down from a nearby tree and slithered across the helicopter's bubble windshield, pausing for a moment before a gust lifted it up and sent it sailing down to the forest below.

Suddenly, Matt sat forward in his chair, his eyes glittering. "I've got it!" The other boys looked at him expectantly as he paused for dramatic effect. "Haunted farm machinery."

Dean arched his eyebrow. "That's better than a ball?"

"Ten times better," Matt said. "It'll have action, adventure, thrills, chills, and," he glanced at Chad, "even a bit of romance." He stood up and headed for the trapdoor.

"Where are you going?" Dean asked.

"To start writing!"

"But aren't we at least going to vote on it?" Dean looked at Chad and Andrew for support.

"Don't ask me," Andrew said. "I'm just the brains of this operation."

"Don't worry, Dean!" Matt called up from below. "I've got the perfect part for you—a starring role!"

Dean's face brightened. "What? For me?" He jumped up and raced toward the trapdoor. "Wait for me!"

6

"Testing, One, Two, Three . . ."

"A girl? You want me to play a girl?" Dean exclaimed, flipping through the script Matt had just handed him. All four boys were sitting in the cafeteria at school.

"Not a girl, a woman," Matt said. "And like I said, it's a starring role."

Dean looked up in anguish. "I realize that, but why do I have to play it?"

"You've got the highest voice."

Dean looked at Chad and Andrew. Chad shrugged. "It's true."

Dean turned back to Matt. "Why don't we get a girl to play it?"

"Like who?" Matt asked.

Dean looked around, and then his face melted with adoration. "Like her."

The other boys followed his gaze until they spotted Matt and Chad's older sister, Joyce, entering the cafeteria with some of her friends. Chad laughed, and Andrew shook his head as Matt rolled his eyes. "No way," Matt said. "Way too bossy. Besides, we have to keep this a secret, from everyone."

Just then, Joyce and a couple of her girlfriends started

toward them.

"Quick!" Matt said. "Hide the scripts!"

The boys stashed their scripts under the table.

"Good afternoon, boys," Joyce said as she approached. "What sort of mischief are you planning today?"

Matt drew an imaginary figure eight on the table with his finger, trying to look as innocent as possible. "Oh, you know, the usual."

Joyce turned to her friends and smirked. "These guys always think they're getting away with something, but they never get away with anything."

The girls giggled.

"That's what you think," Matt said, his face reddening. "You don't know what you don't know."

Joyce arched her eyebrow. "That makes no sense."

"Maybe not to you."

Joyce flicked her hair. "Well, I'll leave you alone now. Wouldn't want to keep you from your reading." She nodded at the papers the boys were hiding under the table, and then she and her friends sashayed away.

"See what I mean?" Matt asked when she was out of earshot. He glanced at Dean, who was enraptured by Joyce's retreating form. "Hey, snap out of it." He gave him a shove.

"Huh? What?" Dean looked as if he was coming back from another world.

The other boys chuckled. Even Matt had to laugh. "Just make sure you read through the script a few times tonight," he said, getting up. "We're recording our first episode tomorrow."

§

The next afternoon, a hastily written sign on Matt and Chad's bedroom door read, "RECORDING! Don't knock. Don't even think about it. Don't care what your reason is. Thanks!"

Inside, the boys were gathered around four microphones, scripts in hand and headphones on, as Andrew made some last-minute adjustments to the sound system. Matt looked around the room, marveling at all the equipment and the wires snaking across the floor. "Man, Andrew, where the heck did you get all this stuff, never mind learn how to use it?"

"I keep my eyes open. Auction sales, moving sales, that sort of thing. Then I experiment with it at home until I figure it out."

"Ever recorded anything before?" Matt asked.

Andrew adjusted a knob and then slipped on his headphones. "A few things. Can you say something into the mic, Chad?"

Chad put his lips up to his microphone and grinned. "Something."

Andrew smiled, but it looked more like a grimace. "Funny. Give me a countdown."

"What kind of things?" Matt asked.

"Five, four, three, two . . .."

Andrew nodded. "Sounds good. Now you, Dean."

"You didn't answer my question," Matt said.

Andrew glanced up. "What?"

"What else have you recorded?"

"Nothing."

"Well, you must have recorded something."

"It doesn't matter. It was just a test. Dean?"

"Do you still have the tape?" Matt pressed.

"Maybe. I don't remember. Dean, can I have your five count?"

Dean stepped up to his mic. "Five—"

"Sorry," Andrew interrupted, "but can you do it as

you're actually going to perform it?"

Dean frowned. "What do you mean?"

"You know, in a girl's voice?"

"Do I have to?"

"Yes, it's the only way I can get the levels right."

Dean sighed, and then, in as high-pitched a voice as possible, he restarted his countdown. "Five, four, three—"

He stopped as Matt broke into hysterical laughter. It spread quickly to Chad, who tried his best to hold it in, but soon both brothers were rolling on the floor. Even Andrew, who was normally rather stoic, was on the verge of cracking up. "Come on, guys," Andrew said, chuckling despite himself. "I'm trying to set the levels here."

Dean tore off his headphones in disgust. "If this is the way things are going to be, I'm out of here."

He headed for the door, but Matt leaped up and blocked his way, still trying to recover from his laughing fit, his eyes glistening with tears of amusement. "I'm sorry, Dean. It'll just take a little getting used to."

"Tell me about it." Dean stomped back to his place at the mic and snatched his headphones off the floor. "Let's just get this over with."

Once everyone had regained control of themselves, Andrew nodded at Dean, and he resumed his countdown. "Five, four, three . . .." The other boys smiled, but they managed to remain silent.

"Sounds good," Andrew said when Dean finished.

"Hey, what's this?" Matt asked, fishing a cassette tape out of a box of spare parts. He held it close to his face so he could read it. "Test session number one." He waved it in the air and looked at Andrew. "Can we listen to it?"

Andrew grabbed for it. "No, I—"

Matt held it just out of reach. "Can we? After all, there's no use going to all this trouble unless we're sure

46

the system works."

"It works," Andrew growled. "I tested it."

"It's not that I don't trust you," Matt continued, "but seeing—or, in this case, hearing—is believing."

Andrew's shoulders sagged. He knew there was no way he was going to get the tape off Matt without a struggle. "Be my guest." He gestured to the tape player that was tied in to the recording system.

Matt popped in the cassette and hit "play." At first, all they heard was a slight hiss. It was followed by Andrew doing a countdown and then clearing his throat. A moment later, he began to sing. "Oh, say can you see, by the dawn's early light, what so proudly we hailed . . .."

"Singing?" Matt exclaimed.

"You actually have a pretty good voice," Chad remarked as Andrew hastened to turn down the volume.

"Yeah, you do," Dean agreed. "But why the American national anthem? Why not 'O Canada'?"

"I don't know. I guess I've always liked the melody."

"Andrew Loewen . . ." Matt shook his head in disbelief. "There's more to you than meets the eye."

"Yeah, like a transformer," Chad said.

"That's right," Matt agreed, grinning. "When you go pro, you can call yourself Optimus Rhyme."

"Good one," Dean said.

"Can we just get back to the recording?" Andrew begged, popping out the test tape and inserting a blank one.

"Okay." Matt put on his game face. "Everyone, take a moment to get settled, and then we'll get started."

§

"Honey, can you believe it's really ours?" Chester, played by Matt, asked.

"It's like a dream come true," replied Maria, voiced by Dean, who spoke in a falsetto. "Our own farm, complete with all the equipment, and the cutest little farmhouse this side of the South Saskatchewan River."

"I hope you know I didn't marry you for your family's money, Maria, but I have to admit that inheriting this from your grandfather is a pretty nice perk."

"I know you better than that, Chester Proudly. You wouldn't marry for anything but love."

Dean turned to the side and pretended to stick his finger down his throat in response to the cheesy dialogue. Matt scowled and motioned for him to smarten up.

"Why don't you go inside and see what you can rustle up for supper while I take a tour through the machine shed?" Chester said. "This equipment looks a bit old, but with a bit of spit and polish, I'm sure I can have it up and running in no time."

"Sounds great, honey," Maria replied. "Don't be too long though. It's a cute little house, but you know how I hate to be alone way out here on the prairie."

With one sneaker on each hand, Andrew made the shoes "walk" in a basin of gravel on the floor, simulating the sound of Chester walking across the yard. He nodded at Chad, who made a wind noise into his mic. Andrew ripped off the shoes and ran a metal bar across a short piece of train rail on the floor, simulating the sound of a machine shop door sliding open. Then Chad held a light switch up to the mic and flicked it.

"Wow, it's like an agricultural museum in here," Chester said. "Look at all this vintage farm equipment."

The shoes back on his hands, Andrew continued to make them "walk" through the gravel.

"I didn't have the heart to tell Maria, but I don't think I can make any of the machinery run. The best we can hope for is to auction it off, along with the rest of the farm, to pay the huge tax bill we just inherited along with it."

Clank. Bonk. Andrew rattled some pieces of machinery in a wooden box.

"What was that?" Chester asked.

More walking through gravel and wind sounds.

"Probably just the building shifting in the wind. Speaking of which, the way it's leaning to the west, it's probably not even safe to be in here. I'd better head back to the house."

Chad poured water from a jug into a saucepan.

"Spaghetti and meat sauce," Maria said. "Chester's favorite."

Chad set the saucepan on a sheet of metal, simulating Maria setting it on the stove.

"If I can just find some candles to put on the table, we'll have the picture-perfect romantic supper in our new place. Let's see if there's some in here."

Chad flicked the light switch a couple of times.

"Hmm . . . that's strange," Maria said. "The light in the pantry must be burnt out. I'll get a match."

Andrew held a box of matches up to the mic and lit one of them.

"There, that's better. Hmm . . . now, where might I find some candles? Maybe on that top shelf over—"

Clunk.

"What was that? Oh, silly me. I dropped the match. I'll have to light another."

Andrew lit another match.

Clunk.

"Chester? Is that you?"

Chad dragged a chain across the metal plate.

Maria gasped. "Chester?"

Andrew "walked" a pair of women's shoes across a

49

piece of wood.

"That's strange," Maria said. "I could have sworn it came from out—"

Clunk.

"Oh! That sounded like it came from upstairs. I wish Chester were here. Maybe I should go get him."

Bang, bang, bang!

Chad pounded the sheet of metal with a hammer.

"Oh, my goodness! Chester!"

Dean's voice cracked on "Chester," prompting a frown from Matt.

"Keep going, we can edit it out," Andrew said, making the women's shoes run across the wood.

"Chester! Where are you? Chester—"

Dean's voice cracked again.

Matt scowled at him. "What's the matter with you?"

Dean shook his head in confusion. "I don't know. I just . . ." He took a deep breath and tried again "Chest—" His voice cracked again.

Just then, the door to Matt and Chad's room flew open, and a familiar figure was silhouetted in the doorway.

Joyce.

7

THE TROUBLE WITH TALENT

"Stop the tape!" Matt tore off his headphones and glared at his sister. "Didn't you read the sign?"

"Of course I read the sign," Joyce said, smiling slyly. "It said not to knock, so, I didn't knock."

Dean squinted at the sign. "She's right, Matt. It says, 'Recording! Don't knock. Don't even—'"

"I know what the sign says. But any sensible person would have realized what it meant."

Joyce smiled. "We are the Taylors, and no one ever accused any of us of being sensible—especially you, Matt."

She looked around her brothers' bedroom, taking in the recording gear as well as the various sound-effect contraptions. "What on earth are you recording in here anyway?" She fixed her gaze on the women's shoes that Andrew was still wearing on his hands. "And are those mine?"

Andrew looked down at the shoes and then ripped them off. "Sorry, Joyce, I—"

"Wait a second, Andrew," Matt said.

Andrew froze.

"We're recording a radio play," Matt continued, "for a class project. And yes, those are your shoes. I'm sorry. Andrew should have asked before he borrowed them."

51

Andrew whirled toward Matt, his eyes ablaze. "But you said—"

"You can join us if you want, Joyce," Dean said, smiling sweetly.

"No, she can't!" Matt glared at Dean, motioning for him to be quiet.

"Why not?" Dean protested. "Then I wouldn't have to play the girl part. You heard what's happening to my voice."

"Which part would you play then?"

"I don't know . . . your part! I want to be the hero for once."

Matt held up his script and smacked it with his other hand. "Then what part would I play?"

"You could just be the director," Chad suggested. "Or the sheriff or the museum curator or the reporter or one of the ghosts."

"What about you and Andrew?" Matt asked. "Those are your parts."

"Well, as you can see," Chad nodded at Andrew, "we kind of have our hands full with the sound effects."

"I didn't mean to start an argument," Joyce said. She turned to Andrew. "You can use the shoes. Just make sure you put them back."

"Thanks," he said quietly.

"As for me playing a part, you can forg—"

"Please?" Dean pleaded, his voice cracking halfway through the word. "I hate playing the girl and, well, you know," he pointed to his throat. "It's not working so well."

Joyce crossed her arms as she stood in the doorway, "What's this for again?"

Matt glanced at the others, mentally urging them to go along with the charade. He'd had a sudden change of heart now that it was clear Dean's voice was unworkable. "It's . . . it's for English class. An end-of-term project."

"Yeah," Andrew said, sounding less than confident. "Uh, forty percent of our mark is riding on this."

"Which is why I'm helping them," Chad added. "I'm not in the class, but I remember how hard it was to get a good mark last year."

"I can't lie to you, Joyce," Dean said, ignoring the scowls from the other guys. "It would mean the world to me to have you be part of it."

Joyce tapped her foot some more, looking at her watch. "How long is this going to take?"

"The episode runs for twenty minutes," Matt replied. "So, if we manage to pull it off in one take, that's it. If we make a few mistakes and have to repeat something, still less than an hour."

"And I'd be playing opposite *him*?" Joyce gestured to Dean, her tone and her body language indicating it was the last thing she wanted to do.

"We can put your microphones on opposite sides of the room," Matt suggested.

"And we'll do your chores for a week," Chad added.

Matt scowled at him.

"Make that a month!" Chad said.

Matt's scowl deepened. He had meant Chad to make the time shorter, not longer.

Joyce nodded silently and then stepped inside and closed the door behind her. "Okay, you have me for an hour. But that's it."

"That's great," Matt said. "Just give us a couple of minutes to get set up, and we can get started. In the meantime, you can look over your script. Dean has one with all your parts marked. Dean?" He looked over at his friend, who was staring at Joyce with a goofy grin on his face. "Dean?"

"Huh, what?" Dean said, snapping out of it.

"Your script? Can you give it to Joyce, please?"

Chad shook his head at the lovesick loon.

"Oh yeah, right. Here you go." Dean handed it to her.

Matt tossed his script to Dean. "Better get reading, 'Chester.' We've got a lot of work to do. Andrew, Chad, be ready in five to take it from the top."

"Got it," Andrew said, already adjusting the recording equipment as Chad rearranged their sound-effects gear.

§

"Oh, Chester, you frightened me," said Maria, now voiced by Joyce. "I swear I heard something up there. A clunking sound, and then banging."

Silence.

Everyone looked at Dean. Instead of reading his part, he was staring lovingly at Joyce. Matt nudged Dean and frantically spun his hand in a circle, indicating he should read his part. Dean nodded and then looked at his script.

"This is an old house, honey." Dean smiled at Joyce when he said the word "honey." She scowled at him and then fixed her eyes on her script. He kept looking at her as he continued. "I'm sure it makes lots of noises. Especially on windy days like today. There's nothing to worry about."

"Cut!" Matt pointed at his script. "The line is, 'There's nothing to be frightened of up there.'"

"That's what I said."

"No, it isn't. If you kept your eyes on the script, you'd know that."

"So what? I improvised."

Matt looked down and took a deep breath before replying. "Dean, I not only wrote this play, I'm also directing it. So if you'll just—"

"Okay, okay, I'll read the script as is. I get it." Dean turned to Joyce and rolled his eyes, pointing his thumb

54

at Matt. "Writers," he said, as if he dealt with them all the time. "So touchy about their work."

"Can we just keep going, please?" Matt pleaded as the other guys chuckled at Dean's obvious attempts to impress Joyce.

Dean gave her a knowing look. "See what I mean?"

"He can be a little exasperating," Joyce agreed, overlooking her dislike of Dean's advances to needle her brother.

"Exactly," Dean replied, giving Matt a look.

Matt groaned in exasperation. "Andrew?"

"Ready."

"Okay. Let's start by redoing Dean's—I mean Chester's—last line."

"Ready in five, four . . .." Andrew did the rest of his countdown silently with his fingers and then pointed at Dean.

Dean cleared his throat. "This an old house, honey," he said in an abnormally low voice. "I'm sure it makes lots of—"

"Cut!"

Andrew sighed and stopped the tape. Chad shook his head in disbelief.

"Dean, what the heck are you doing?" Matt asked.

"What do you mean? I was just—"

"Your voice. Why is it so low?"

Dean cleared his throat again and lowered his pitch. "You know, that's just how my voice is. Low. Like thunder rumbling across the prairies." Even Joyce had to giggle at that.

"No, it isn't," Matt said. "That's why we had you reading Maria's part just moments ago, remember?"

Dean put his hands on his hips. "And how well did that go, huh? And don't blame me; that was a casting problem, not a performance issue. You should have known my voice was starting to change." He looked at Joyce. "I don't know about you, but I'm starting to lose confidence in our director."

Joyce nodded, playing along with Dean. "He does seem a bit testy."

Matt clenched his fists in frustration. "Can we just get through this scene?"

Dean glanced at Joyce. She smiled and nodded, enjoying the opportunity to push her brother's buttons. Meanwhile, Matt looked like he wanted to strangle Dean.

"Okay, Matt, no need to have a hissy fit," Dean said. "We'll read the script exactly as written, keeping our voices the same, right Joyce?"

She gave him a thumbs-up, trying not to laugh.

Dean turned back to Matt. "I was just trying to give you some options."

"Options?" Matt asked, flabbergasted.

"Yeah, you know, when you edit this thing."

"I don't want options," Matt said. "I want you to read every line exactly the same each time in exactly the same voice. This is a radio play, remember? The listeners can't see you. If you suddenly use a different voice, people will think it's a different character. Got it?"

"But what if Chester became possessed by the ghosts, and that's why he's suddenly talking like that, only Maria doesn't notice, at least not at first. Have you ever considered that option? I really think you should." He smiled at Joyce, hoping to impress her with his creative contribution.

"Would you just read your lines?" Matt shouted.

Dean gave Matt a mock salute and then rolled his eyes. "Aye, aye, skipper. Sheesh."

§

Ninety minutes later, Matt and Chad's bedroom door opened, and the four boys and Joyce filed out. Matt looked exhausted. Dean was beaming.

"Sorry it took longer than I expected, Joyce," Matt said, glaring at Dean. "But sometimes the 'talent' can be difficult to manage."

"That's okay," Joyce said. "It was actually kind of fun. But remember, you guys promised to do my chores. And if you get a good mark, you still owe me. Big time."

"We certainly do," Chad replied, silently indicating the others should show their gratitude.

"Yeah, thanks, Joyce," Andrew said. "You were great."

"Yeah," Matt agreed. "And you didn't even get a chance to rehearse."

"Simply divine," Dean said. "Especially that part—"

"We'll let you know when we finish editing," Matt interrupted, dragging Dean toward the kitchen.

8

BACK TO THE MARSH

It was a beautiful Saturday morning in late May as the boys pedaled their bikes down the gravel road leading to the Milligan Creek Heritage Marsh. The sky was a deep-blue dome streaked with a few wisps of white cloud. The slight breeze was warm on their faces, carrying the scent of the emerald-green fields of wheat, canola, barley, and flax they passed along the way, the crops already nearly a foot high.

"We should be out playing baseball," Dean huffed as he stood up and pedaled hard to keep up with the others. He was on a BMX, and they were on ten speeds, which allowed them to change gears to accommodate for the wind. He was stuck with a single gear.

"Baseball can wait," Matt said. "We've got way bigger fish to fry."

"What are we gonna tell Henrietta?" Chad asked.

"Nothing!" Matt said. "Just that we wanna look at some ducks. Did you remember your binoculars, Andy?"

Andrew patted his shoulder. "In my pack, along with a copy of 'A Field Guide to Western Birds.' I found it on my dad's bookshelf."

Matt grinned. "Nice touch! It's the perfect cover!"

"Why are we doing this in the daylight?" Dean asked. "If we came at night, we wouldn't need a cover story."

Chad looked back at Dean over his shoulder. "Trespassing, remember?"

"Oh yeah. But what if she suspects something?"

"There's nothing to suspect," Matt said. "First, we'll keep a low profile. Maybe she won't even notice us. If we do have to talk to her, I'll just tell her we're four amateur bird watchers who were so taken by our recent tour of the marsh that we had to come back for a second look, to see if we can spot that yellow-headed merchandiser, or whatever it was."

"Red-breasted merganser," Andrew said.

"Whatever. I'll just tell her we want a sticker."

"On second thought, maybe we should let Andrew do the talking," Chad said. "At least he knows something about birds."

"Don't worry, I can wing it," Matt quipped, grinning at the others to make sure they caught his pun.

Dean groaned. "Lame-o."

"Shh . . . we're almost there," Chad said. "And there she is!"

The boys fell silent as they pulled up to the yellow tubular steel gate, which Henrietta was in the process of unlocking. She looked up at them in surprise and then smiled. "Good morning! And what sort of mischief might you young whippoorwills be up to today?"

The boys exchanged nervous glances. Was she onto them already?

"We're here to look at birds, ma'am." Matt gestured at Andrew. "Our friend here got a sticker the other day during our school field trip, and now the rest of us want one."

"Nothing like a little friendly competition to get the blood flowing, hey, boys? Just what I like to see. I'm just getting started for the day, but the birds have been at it since sunrise, not to mention the muskrats! Come in, come in!" She swung the gate open. "Make yourself at home. There's a bike rack beside the interpretive center. Feel free to wander wherever you like. Do you have some binoculars?"

"Yes," Andrew said. "And a field guide."

"Which one?"

"A Field Guide to Western Birds."

"By Robert Tory Peterson?"

"Uh, I think so."

"Can I see it?"

"Sure."

Andrew dug the book out of his pack and handed it to her. It was a light-blue hardcover embossed with the title and a picture of a swallow.

"Ah, a nineteen sixty-one version," she said, flipping through it. "Do you have the dust jacket?"

Andrew nodded. "Yes, but I left it at home. I didn't want to damage it."

"Very wise. You know, I have a nineteen forty-one copy at home, a first edition. Signed by Peterson himself. Very rare. He hardly ever signs books anymore. I never take it into the field though. Too valuable. For a birdwatcher, this is like the Bible. Treat it as such, son. Read it, study it, memorize it." She snapped it shut and handed it back to Andrew. "That goes for all of you."

"Uh, yes, ma'am," Andrew said.

"Now, let me see your specs."

"Excuse me?"

"Your lenses, your binoculars. Cough 'em up."

"Oh." Andrew pulled them out of his pack and handed them to her.

"Very nice, very nice," she said, turning them over

61

in her hands. "Nikon wide field eight by thirty-fives. I've been saving up for a pair of these myself."

"My dad's a hunter, and—"

"Shh . . ." Henrietta put a hand on Andrew's arm and held a finger to her lips. "We don't use that word around here," she whispered. "Disturbs the birds."

"Uh, sorry," Andrew murmured.

"No worries," Henrietta said a little too loudly, looking around as if she were speaking for the birds' benefit. "No harm, no fowl, get it?" She clapped Andrew on the back. "Okay, off you go! I can't stand around talking to you boys all day. I'm hard at work on the script for my next radio broadcast. I can't wait to share it with the world! But first, I need to do my morning rounds."

She walked off toward the boardwalk, humming.

"So much for keeping a low profile," Chad whispered once she was gone.

"I knew we should have come later," Dean replied. "If something goes wrong, she's going to know it was us."

"No, she won't," Matt said. "She loves us—especially bird boy here," he added, pointing at Andrew. "We're the last people she would suspect."

"What do we do now?" Chad asked.

"Divide and conquer," Matt replied. "And hurry. We need to get it in place before she finishes her rounds. Dean, you and Chad take the binoculars and the bird book, and pretend you're looking for that blue-footed marmalute."

"Red-breasted—"

"I don't care what it's called, Dean!" Matt handed Chad a walkie-talkie, also pulling out one for himself. "We'll keep in touch with these. If we need you to create a distraction, I'll let you know."

"A distraction?" Dean asked, looking around. "What kind of distraction?"

"You'll think of something. Now let's go!"

With one eye on Henrietta, Matt and Andrew ducked low enough so they were hidden by the bulrushes and then raced toward the interpretive center—and the radio tower.

Dean looked at Chad. "What do we do now?"

"Look for birds, I guess. Want the binoculars?"

"Sure." Dean took them from Chad, and then the two of them wandered off toward the boardwalk. As they walked, Chad flipped through the field guide.

"You know, this book is pretty cool. Imagine how long it took to paint all these pictures."

"All those were done by one guy?"

"Yup."

"Wow. He must really love birds. Even more than what's her name."

"Henrietta?"

"Yeah."

"Speaking of which," Chad said, "there she is."

Dean looked up and saw Henrietta starting up the stairs on the observation platform. He glanced back at the interpretive center, where Matt and Andrew were just approaching the radio tower. "That isn't good."

"You're right," Chad said, pulling out his walkie-talkie as he started toward her. "Time for a distraction!"

§

"Where are we going to put it?" Matt asked, staying low and keeping an eye out for Henrietta.

"I don't know," Andrew said. "That's something I've been worried about."

The boys examined the tower base. It was made of crisscrossing metal beams bolted to a cement pad, leaving nowhere to hide the Hijacker.

"Can we bury it?" Matt suggested.

"We could, but I didn't think to bring a shovel."

"What about—"

"Mayday, mayday!" Chad shouted over the walkie-talkie.

"Duck!" Matt slammed Andrew to the ground before he could respond.

§

Henrietta had just reached the top of the observation tower when Dean and Chad jogged up.

"Ms. Blunt!" Chad called between breaths.

She gazed around in confusion.

"Down here!" Dean said.

She looked down at them and smiled. "Well, hello, boys. What's your hurry?"

"We just saw a . . ." Chad paused to catch his breath. "We just saw a . . ."

Dean grabbed the book from him and flipped it open to a random page. "A northern flicker!"

"Really?" she said. "In the marsh? That's a member of the woodpecker family, and there are no trees around here. I sure hope he hasn't started pecking holes in my interpretive center. Where did you—"

"Down here!" Dean said, trying desperately to keep her from turning toward the interpretive center and seeing Matt and Andrew. "I mean, can you come down here for a second and look at this hole? Maybe you can tell if a woodpecker made it."

"A woodpecker? On my tower? Let me see it!"

She hurried back down the stairs.

"What hole?" Chad hissed, turning to Dean.

"I don't know. Find one!"

§

Fifteen minutes later, the boys reconvened at the entrance to the marsh, all of them a bit shaken.

"Did you find a place to hide it?" Chad asked.

Andrew nodded. "Yes. Just took a bit longer than expected. Thanks for holding her off."

"I never want to hear about another bird again," Dean lamented. "She got me to volunteer to come back and help paint the observation tower with a special paint that will keep woodpeckers away, all thanks to this stupid book." He handed the field guide and the binoculars back to Andrew.

Matt clapped Dean on the shoulder. "Way to take one for the team."

"So, where'd you put it?" Chad asked.

Matt glanced at Andrew, and both boys grinned. "Right where she'd least expect it," Matt said.

9

THE GRAVEYARD SHIFT

Two empty pizza boxes hung open, their insides littered with half-chewed crusts and surrounded by several empty pop cans on the tree house table. The smell of pepperoni, mushrooms, and cheese still hung in the air as the boys rolled out their sleeping bags on the bunk beds in preparation for their overnight listening party. Matt had taken to calling it "the graveyard shift," named after the work shift that takes place from late evening to early morning in a factory.

"You know, that's what we should have called our radio show," Chad said. "'The Graveyard Shift.' The title alone sounds scary."

"That's what we can call the sequel," Matt replied.

"Sequel?" Dean asked in surprise. "You're already planning a sequel?"

Matt grinned. "I'm always planning a sequel."

"I don't know," Andrew said. "We don't tend to do too well around graveyards." He glanced up at his makeshift canoe paddle from their voyage down Milligan Creek, which they had mounted on the wall as a memento of their adventure.

Matt opened their mini-fridge and bent down to peer

inside. "Anyone for another pop?" He pulled out a can of Pepsi and cracked it open. "You're going to be thankful for that caffeine kick."

"Caffeine is the last thing you need, Matt." Dean checked his watch. "Besides, it's almost midnight. We only need to stay up for another half hour until the program's done."

"I'll be way too buzzed to sleep after that," Matt replied, taking another slug.

"Tell me about it," Chad said.

Matt wiped his mouth with the back of his hand. "Are you sure you set that timer properly, Andrew?"

"Yes, for the hundredth time," Andrew grumbled, although he couldn't help from glancing at his watch. "But it wouldn't hurt to turn the radio on now."

"Okay, but keep the volume low until our show starts," Matt said. "There's only so much of Ms. Blunt's warbling a man can take."

Andrew turned up the radio as the other boys gathered around it like a family in the pre-television era, staring at the radio as they listened, even though there was nothing to see.

". . . although a lot of great work has been done and many research questions have been answered," Henrietta said on the radio, "we still have a lot to learn about how waterfowl and other kinds of birds react to habitat—" Her voice was cut off by a burst of static, followed by silence.

"Dead air!" Dean said. "Every radio station's worst nightmare!"

"That's another great name for a radio show," Chad said, "hey, Matt? 'Dead Air.'"

Matt was too amped up to respond. He looked at Andrew. "What's happening? Where's our show?"

Matt's question was answered by his own voice on the radio. In addition to filling out a few minor roles in the program, they had also added him as narrator to help set the scene.

"Ladies and gentlemen," he began as spooky music played in the background, another element Andrew had added during editing, "humankind is an intelligent species, a powerful species, an innovative and inventive species, able to plumb the ocean's depths and scan the far reaches of outer space. But human beings are also proud creatures, prone to think too highly of themselves, to believe they are capable of anything. But wherever the light of human knowledge shines, it can't help but create shadows, murky pockets of ignorance, mystery, and fear."

Chad turned to Matt. "Hey, that's pretty good. Did you write that?"

"No, he did," Matt said, gesturing at Andrew. "Shh!"

"Within these shadows, hidden forces are at work in our world, dark forces," Matt's voice continued, "malevolent powers that will not be ignored." The music shifted to an even darker tone, a low bass rumble that made the timbers in the tree house vibrate. "Every so often, these forces manifest themselves in a powerful way as a reminder, a warning, that we ignore them . . . at our peril."

Dean clutched his pillow to his chest. "Oh, man, I'm scared already."

Matt scowled at him. "Shh . . .."

"We are about to witness a manifestation of these powers, a dark omen that we and the characters in our story would do well to heed. It all begins on a farm, a seemingly ordinary farm of golden wheat fields rolling in the breeze, ready for the harvest. But as Chester Proudly and his new wife, Maria, are about to learn, this farm is anything but ordinary, and beneath those fields lies a terrible secret that is about to be unleashed in the first episode of 'It Came . . . from the Grain'!"

The music reached a crescendo and then faded out, replaced by the sound of a breeze, crickets chirping, and birds singing.

"Honey, can you believe this farm is really ours?" Chester asked.

"It's like a dream come true," Maria replied.

"This is awesome!" Chad exclaimed. "It sounds totally professional! Great work, Andrew!"

Andrew smiled bashfully. "Thanks."

"Would you guys be quiet?" Dean pleaded. "I can't hear Joyce!"

The other boys looked at him for a moment, and then, as if obeying a silent cue, they all pummeled him with their pillows.

§

The following Monday at school, the guys could hardly concentrate, giddy with excitement about the success of their first broadcast. One question lingered in their minds: had anyone heard it?

To find out, they made sure to eavesdrop on every conversation possible, straining to overhear any mention of their show. But all their efforts earned them were a few strange looks and some outright demands to get lost.

Discouraged, Matt shoved his books into his locker at noon and grabbed his lunch, ready to head down to the cafeteria.

"Moo."

The voice came from behind, startling him. He turned around. It was Ben, the kid who had asked about cows in the marsh, bedhead and all.

"Hey, Ben," Matt said glumly. "You scared me."

"Cows aren't scary."

"No, but you can be—sometimes." Matt nodded at Ben's hair. "You know, with a little water and a comb, you could almost—"

"You know what's really scary?" Ben continued, as if Matt hadn't spoken.

"No, what?"

"What I heard on the radio on Saturday night."

"Oh yeah?" Matt felt a rush of excitement shoot through him. "What was that?"

"I don't know exactly. I only caught part of it. Something about ghosts. Haunted farm machinery. A terrible secret."

"Sounds cool. What station?"

"That's the really scary part. It was on the Wetlands Unlimited station. I like to listen to it at night. Ms. Blunt's voice puts me to sleep."

Matt nodded. "Tell me about it."

"But not that night. It didn't put me to sleep at all. It kept me up super late, and I slept in half the morning. My mom thought I was sick, but I told her—hey, where are you going?"

"Sorry to hear about your rotten night, Ben!" Matt said as he hurried down the hall. "But I forgot I had an important meeting!"

§

Moments later, Matt arrived in the cafeteria, breathless. He spotted Chad, Dean, and Andrew sitting on the far side of the room, their heads hanging in discouragement as they munched their sandwiches. "Hey, guess what?" Matt said, running up to them.

"You forgot your lunch?" Chad asked. "Don't worry; Mom packed me an extra sandwich." He held it out to his brother, but Matt pushed it away as he sat down and

71

plunked his brown lunch bag on the table.

"No, dummy. Something way better." Matt glanced around and then leaned in close, lowering his voice to a whisper. "Someone listened to our show!"

Immediately, all three boys brightened. "They did?" Dean asked. "Who?"

"Ben. Look, there he is now."

All four boys watched as Ben made his way through the cafeteria, apparently still in somewhat of a daze from lack of sleep. He took a seat by himself and opened his lunch bag, the rooster tails in his hair waving about.

"So?" Dean pressed. "What did he say?"

"He only heard part of it, but it scared the heck out of him. He was up half the night!"

"Cool!" Chad said, his eyes wide with excitement.

"I know," Matt replied. "And it gave me an idea."

"Uh oh." Dean leaned back in his chair. "I hate when that happens."

"No, hear me out. There's no point in continuing the series if only one person has heard the first episode."

"So, what are you saying?" Chad asked.

"We replay it this Saturday night. We can sneak in, rewind the tape, and reset the timer, right, Andrew?"

Andrew nodded as he chewed his sandwich. "Sure."

"But before we do that," Matt continued, "we do something we should have done all along."

Dean's eyes narrowed with suspicion. "What's that?"

Matt grinned. "Advertise!"

10

THE DANGER ZONE

After school the following day, the hallways of Milligan Creek Composite School were empty and quiet. Only the janitor remained, shuffling from classroom to classroom with his mop, bucket, and tool cart, a pair of Sony Walkman earphones on his head.

Careful to stay out of sight, four figures slunk down the hall, shoving slips of paper into the air vents of each locker as they went.

"I still think this is a bad idea," Dean whispered. "What if these fall into the wrong hands?"

"All they say is the radio station frequency and the date and time people should tune in," Matt said. "There's no way anyone can link them back to us."

"Careful, he's coming out!" Chad called.

The boys slipped into the science lab. It had two long counters equipped with goose-necked faucets, Bunsen burners, and lab stools, and it smelled faintly of formaldehyde. They waited until the janitor passed, singing along with the song on his Walkman. "Don't forget me when I'm gone . . . my heart would break . . . ." The boys grinned at his terrible voice, augmented by the cart's squeaky wheels, which, oddly enough, were almost in time with the music.

A moment later, Matt peeked out. "Coast is clear!" He ran out of the lab, the other boys right behind him, and raced up the stairs to the senior grades' floor.

"What if we get trapped up here?" Dean asked.

"There's two ways down," Matt replied. "If the janitor comes up one way, we'll go down the other. Now hurry. The sooner we get this done, the better."

The boys hustled down the hall, shoving a slip of paper into each locker.

"Do you really think people will tune in?" Dean asked.

"Not all of them," Chad replied, "but some will."

They were nearly finished when a mechanical whirring sound filled the hallway. Matt looked around, perplexed. "What's that?"

"The elevator!" Andrew said, pointing to the elevator door, which was halfway down the hall. It had been installed recently to facilitate physically challenged students and staff. "He must be using it to bring up his cleaning cart!"

"This way!" Matt led the boys to the end of the hall opposite from where they had come up. He pushed on the bar that should have opened one of the double doors leading to the other staircase, but instead, he slammed into the door when the bar refused to budge. The other boys crashed into him in their haste to escape.

"Try the other one!" Chad cried, looking back over his shoulder with fear.

Matt pushed on it. "It's locked too!"

"What do we do?" Dean asked.

"In here!" Matt opened the door to a classroom at the end of the hall. The moment the boys were inside, the elevator doors opened.

"What do we do now?" Dean whispered. "It's only a matter of time before he comes in here to clean!"

"I'm thinking, I'm thinking," Matt said, his eyes darting around the room. It was essentially a cinder-block box, furnished with a teacher's desk at the back, five rows of student desks, chalkboards, and a row of windows along the outside wall.

Chad stood by the door and listened. "He's coming this way!"

The other boys paused and listened. The telltale squeak of the cart approaching was unmistakable.

"What do we do?" Dean asked, on the verge of tears.

§

Moments later, the janitor wheeled his cleaning cart into the classroom, singing along with the song on his Walkman. "Highway to the danger zone, uh-mm-mmm-mm-mmm . . ." He paused to play his mop like an air guitar. Then he spotted something on the floor: a bundle of paper slips held together by a rubber band. He flipped through them and then stuck them into his pocket, resuming his air guitar playing. "Ride into the danger zone, uh-mm-mmm-mm-mmm . . ."

He straightened a few desks and was about to start sweeping when he noticed one of the windows was open. He went over to it, looked out, and then slid it shut and locked it, not missing a beat of his song. "Headin' into twilight, spreading out her wings tonight . . .."

§

Outside, the boys crouched on a flat roof about eight feet below the window the janitor had just locked.

"That was close," Chad said.

"Too close," Dean replied. "The question is, how do we

get down from here?"

"Don't worry; I know a way," Matt said.

Dean rolled his eyes. "Of course you do." He was about to follow the other boys when he stopped and felt his pockets, searching for something. "Wait a second. My papers! The janitor must have them!"

They all looked up at the window. "It's too late to worry about that," Matt said. "Come on!"

They raced across the roof, keeping low to avoid being seen by passing cars. Then they jumped down to a lower roof and shinnied down a drainpipe to the ground.

Just as they were dusting themselves off, a police cruiser rounded the corner. The boys froze, terrified.

"Do you think he saw us?" Chad whispered.

As if in answer to his question, the cruiser stopped.

"Oh no," Dean said. "We're so dead."

The policeman lowered his window.

"What do we do?" Chad whispered.

"Just act natural," Matt said.

"You mean terrified?" Dean asked. "Because that feels really natural right now!"

"Shh . . .," Chad said through clenched teeth.

"Good afternoon, officer," Matt said as he approached the police cruiser.

"Hello, Matt," Staff Sergeant Richard Romanowski replied. "What are you boys doing on school property so late in the afternoon?"

Originally from Kitchener, Ontario, Staff Sergeant Romanowski had been posted as the head of the RCMP detachment in Milligan Creek for three years. In his early forties, he was a tough but fair-minded policeman with a full mustache that was probably the envy of RCMP officers everywhere.

"Oh, you know, just stirring up mischief," Matt said.

Dean's eyes widened with fear at Matt's seemingly foolish admission.

"I'll bet you were, if past experience is any indicator." A faint smile emerged from behind Romanowski's crumb catcher. "Do I have to run you boys downtown and interrogate you, or do you want to confess right now?"

"We want to confess!" Dean blurted, earning hard looks from the other boys.

"Oh, really . . .." A ghost of suspicion lurked in Romanowski's eyes. "To what?"

"To . . . having no idea what you're talking about?" Dean ventured.

As the staff sergeant studied his face, Dean did his best to smile, but it looked more like the kind of grimace on a cheap Halloween mask meant to scare little kids.

"What he means is, we were just hanging around, trying to come up with a good end-of-school prank," Chad said. "Nothing harmful. Just fun."

Romanowski nodded slowly, clearly smelling a rat but unable to pin it down. "You boys happen to have any spray paint on you?" His eyes did a quick visual search of them.

Matt held up his hands innocently, looking at his buddies as they did the same. "It doesn't appear that way."

"We've had some trouble with graffiti on the school lately. You boys know anything about that?"

"We've heard about it, sir, and we've seen some of it, but we'd never do anything like that," Matt replied.

"I didn't think so," Romanowski said, the suspicion receding from his eyes. "Well, if you do hear anything, be sure to tell your teachers—or me."

"Yes, sir," Matt said. "Definitely."

"As for end-of-school pranks, a word of advice . . ." The boys tensed as Romanowski's words lingered in the late-afternoon air. "Don't get caught." He winked and then rolled up his window and drove away.

The boys remained in place until the cruiser turned right onto Main Street. Then all four of them collapsed onto the ground.

"Now *that* was close," Andrew said.

"Tell me about it," Matt replied. He reached into his pocket and pulled out one of the slips advertising the radio show. "Let's just hope these little babies work."

11

Fans!

Just before midnight on the following Saturday, the boys were assembled once again in the tree house, eager to hear the repeat broadcast. Dean could barely keep his eyes open, having spent the day "volunteering" to help Henrietta stain the observation tower with woodpecker-proof paint.

"Oh, my arms," he groaned as he flopped onto a lower bunk. "I don't know if I'll ever be able to use them again. Who would have thought saving the wetlands could be so painful?"

The only good part about it was that the distraction of Dean being at Henrietta's side had allowed Andrew to sneak in and rewind the tape, setting the timer for it to replay that evening.

"Are you sure the battery's still good?" Chad asked. "It's been sitting out there for a week."

"I swapped that as well," Andrew said. "Just in case."

"Good thinking." Matt looked at his watch. "It's just about time."

He turned up the volume on the radio. Right on cue, they heard the tell-tale burst of static, followed by Matt's voice introducing the show, which he did at the start of every episode. Matt cocked his head to the side as he listened. "Hey, something sounds different." He listened a little longer. "Something *is* different. That doesn't sound like me." He turned to Andrew. "What happened?" He was surprised to find Andrew barely suppressing a grin.

"Precautions," Andrew said.

"What do you mean?" Chad asked.

"Well, we're going to a wider audience now—at least that's what we hope—so, I thought it might be a good idea to disguise our voices a bit, adjust the pitch and a few other things, just in case someone might recognize us."

"That's brilliant!" Matt said. "Why didn't you tell us that earlier?"

"I wanted to see if you'd notice. Our little run-in with Staff Sergeant Romanowski the other day is what made me think of it."

"Well, it sounds like it worked." Matt listened for a moment. "I don't even recognize myself."

"There's just one problem," Dean said.

Andrew turned toward him. "What's that?"

"I was so looking forward to hearing Joyce's beautiful, melodic voice."

The other guys looked at each other, nodded, and then started pounding Dean with pillows.

"Hey, cut it out!" Dean cried. "My arms! My arms!"

§

The boys couldn't wait for the weekend to be over so they could get to school and hear the response to their show. Worse, they weren't even able to spend Sunday together worrying about it, each of them occupied with a family obligation, church, or chores.

When Monday morning finally arrived, Matt and Chad were so excited that they woke up nearly an hour earlier than usual and were ready long before their bus was due to arrive.

"Look at these eager young scholars," Mr. Taylor said as he entered the kitchen half an hour later. Matt and Chad were sitting at the kitchen table, their backpacks beside them. "What's the hurry, boys?"

"No hurry," Matt said. "It's just getting light earlier and earlier. The sun must've woken us up."

Chad nodded. "Yep, that must be it."

Mr. Taylor gave them a skeptical look as he put a couple of pieces of bread in the toaster. "A likely story."

"What?" Matt asked, appearing insulted. "Is it a crime to wake up early?"

Mr. Taylor paused, about to open the fridge. "For most people? No. For you two?"

Suddenly, Matt looked out the window. "Bus is here. Gotta go!" He and Chad grabbed their backpacks and ran out the door.

Mr. Taylor chuckled and then opened the fridge. A moment later, he stuck his head around the door. "Honey, are we out of Cheez Whiz?"

§

As soon as Chad and Matt set foot on the bus, they heard their fellow passengers buzzing about something. As they listened, they realized everyone was talking about the same thing: their show!

"What'd you think about that part where the possessed swather took out the nosy reporter?" a boy near the front of the bus said.

"It sounded disgusting," his friend replied. "I wonder how they created that sound effect."

Matt grinned at Chad, who had created the sound by

whipping a slab of raw beef with a stick.

"I'm just glad it wasn't the rock picker," another boy chimed in.

"Or the baler," another added. "That would have been really ugly. Who would have thought farm machinery could be so deadly?"

Chad and Matt took a seat by Andrew, who had gotten on a few stops before them.

"This is crazy!" Matt whispered.

"I know!" Andrew replied, his face uncharacteristically animated. "I think they all listened to it!"

"Sounds like they loved it too," Chad said.

"Yup."

"Moo."

All three boys looked up to find Ben peering over the seat in front of them, bedhead and all.

"Hi, Ben," Matt said, trying to act casual. "How was your weekend?"

"Terrible," Ben replied. "They played that radio show again, and this time I listened to the whole thing."

"And?"

"There wasn't one cow in the entire show, even though it's set on a farm. That and I just found out we're moving to town this summer."

Matt glanced at his buddies. "Well, maybe they're going to put one in a future episode. Sorry about the move, by the way."

"I sure hope so." Ben retreated to his seat, but not before casting a final "Moo" over his shoulder.

The three friends grinned at each other, and then Matt turned to Andrew. "What else have you heard?"

"Everyone seems to like it. And get this: Some of the girls are in love with Chester!"

"What?" Matt exclaimed. "That was supposed to be

my role."

"It's his voice," Andrew said. "They say he sounds dreamy."

"Oh boy." Chad slid down into his seat. "We'd better not tell Dean that."

"No kidding," Matt replied. Then he looked up. "Listen, the girls across the aisle are talking about it."

As soon as all three boys turned their heads toward them, the girls stopped talking and glared at them.

"Can we help you with something, *boys*?" Glenda, a girl with thick glasses, asked.

Matt gave her a sick grin and then pretended to look elsewhere.

"Anyway," Glenda continued, "if I were married to Chester Proudly—"

"Dream on!" her friend said. All three girls giggled.

Matt couldn't help but smack his forehead as he turned to his friends. "There's no way we can tell Dean about this!"

§

At school the same pattern repeated itself. This time, the boys didn't have to go out of their way to eavesdrop. Everyone was talking about the show.

"This is incredible," Matt said as he, Chad, and Andrew gathered near his locker during a break later that morning. "We're famous—at least our show is."

"I know," Dean said, walking up. "You should hear what the girls are saying about my voice! They think I'm dreamy—thanks to Andrew."

Matt grabbed Dean's arm. "You didn't tell them it was you, did you?"

"You think I'm nuts?" Dean pushed Matt away. "My

83

mom would kill me if she found out we hijacked that crazy marsh lady's radio signal. Speaking of which, I'm supposed to volunteer there again this Saturday." He put his hand on his shoulder and rotated it to work out the stiffness. "I don't know if I'm going to survive." Then he paused as a thought struck him. "I wonder if Joyce heard it."

"I doubt it," Matt replied. "We had to jump out the window before we could put any of our flyers into her grade's lockers, remember?"

"Oh yeah."

Matt looked around nervously. "It's great so many people listened to the show, but now I'm paranoid someone's going to find out we're the ones behind it."

Chad looked at him in surprise. "Really? *You're* worried? That's a first."

"I'm the ringleader. I've got the most to lose." No sooner were the words out of Matt's mouth than he noticed a crowd forming at the end of the hall. "Hey, what's that?"

As the boys moved closer, they realized it was one of their classmates, Darryl, a natural-born entrepreneur. Even though he was only in junior high, he was already trading stocks, having recently invested in a new computer software company called Microsoft.

"Don't worry if you missed the show, because I have it right here, a limited edition, first ever episode of 'It Came . . . from the Grain'! Just two dollars each."

Kids were lining up to buy it from him.

Dean looked at his friends in shock. "Why didn't we think of that?"

Andrew nodded in agreement. "Definitely a lost revenue opportunity."

Matt scanned the hallway, taking it all in. "You know what this means, right?"

Chad clapped his hands in anticipation. "Time to record our next episode!"

§

After school that day, the boys converged at Matt and Chad's house, scripts in hand.

"Feel free to get something to eat," Matt said, grabbing a cookie in the kitchen on the way to his and Chad's bedroom. "I'm just going to drop off my things and then see if Joyce—"

He stopped short when he opened his bedroom door. Inside, Joyce was sitting in his desk chair, and she looked furious.

12

REWRITES

"You said it was for a school project," Joyce said through clenched teeth.

"It was!" Matt replied. "I mean, at least it—"

"You hijacked the Wetlands Unlimited radio signal?"

"Hijacked is such a harsh word. More like—"

"Stole? Commandeered? Seized? Captured?"

Matt frowned. "What are you, a walking thesaurus?"

"Who are you talking to?" Dean asked, coming up behind him. As soon as he saw Joyce, he smiled—until he realized she wasn't smiling.

"Hello, *dreamy*," Joyce said, her voice dripping with angry sarcasm.

Dean swallowed hard. "Uh, I think I forgot my milk in the kitchen." He held up his half-eaten oatmeal chocolate chip cookie. "Be right back." He retreated from the doorway as quickly as possible.

§

"We've got trouble," Dean said to Andrew and Chad as soon as he returned to the kitchen.

Chad set down his glass of milk and wiped his mouth. "What's wrong?"

"Joyce," Dean stage-whispered, jabbing his thumb back toward the boys' bedroom.

Chad led the others as they crept back to listen in.

§

"Joyce, it's a huge hit," Matt said. "You should hear people talking—"

"I did hear them," Joyce replied. "That's all I heard about all day."

Matt's eyes widened with fear. "You didn't tell anyone it was us, did you?"

"Of course not."

His shoulders relaxed. "Good."

"I would never admit to being part of this!" She held up the script.

"I understand, Joyce, we should have—"

"At least not without some serious rewrites."

He looked at her in surprise. "What?"

She flipped through the pages. "Your act two? No offense, but it's atrocious. In fact, it's hardly there. And the climax? What's with all the kissing? I thought this was a horror story, not 'Pretty in Pink.'"

"That was my idea," Dean said, holding his hand up as he poked his head around the doorway.

"Figures," Joyce said. "Anyway, if you boys want me to continue to be part of your little show, we've got some serious work to do."

Matt looked at the other guys as they trickled into the room, sensing Joyce's wrath had retreated. "Well, come on then," he said. "Let's get started!"

§

Hours later, the boys emerged from Chad and Matt's bedroom looking weary and browbeaten, but Joyce was still bursting with energy. "This is going to be great, guys," she said, slapping her script with the back of her hand. "Just make sure you all memorize your parts."

"You weren't kidding about the bossy part," Dean whispered to Matt, his eyes bloodshot.

"I heard that!" Joyce said.

Dean's face turned red. "Sorry!"

§

"Quick, this way!" Chester shouted, an engine roar growing in the distance. "We'll hide in this grain field!"

He and Maria ran into the wheat field, the tall, ripe grain slapping at their bodies as they struggled through it.

"It's like trying to run through waist-deep water!" Maria cried.

"I know. Here, take my hand!"

"I still don't understand," Maria said as they continued to run. "Who's trying to kill us?"

"I don't know," Chester replied. "But I'm going to find out. You wait here. I'll be right back."

"No, don't leave me!"

"It'll be okay!" Chester said, his voice fading into the distance. "Just stay put!"

Chester raced through the grain. "There it is! I see the headlights. Just have to get behind it before whoever's driving that combine sees me."

Finally, Chester came to a stop. "There. Now, if I just crouch down here and wait."

The roar of the combine grew louder.

"Hold on a second. I need some kind of weapon. There, a rock. It'll have to do."

The combine was nearly upon him, the sound of its engine deafening.

"If I can catch the ladder as it drives past . . . There, just got it. Now to find out who's driving this thing."

Chester's feet clanged on the ladder as he climbed up to the cab. A click and a bang sounded as he unlatched the door to the combine's cab and flung it open. "All right you—what? The cab is empty! Then how—"

Suddenly, someone—or something—gunned the combine's engine.

"The combine is turning. But how? Need to grab the wheel." He grunted as he strained to turn it. "It won't budge. And it's heading right for . . . Maria!"

Maria huffed, still trying to catch her breath after their run through the field. "I wish Chester wouldn't have left me here. Wait a second, the combine, it's changed direction. Maybe if I peek over the grain . . . the headlights, they're coming right for me! Have to run . . . it's no use, no matter which way I turn, it follows. Chester!"

In the cab, Chester released the steering wheel, pushed every button, and pulled every lever. "I've got to be able to shut this thing down somehow, but nothing's working! Wait a second, the key. It's not even in the ignition! But how—no, Maria!" He pounded on the combine's windshield. "Maria, look out!" he shouted. "She's not going to make it! Somebody stop this thing!"

Maria screamed as the combine bore down on her, but her cry was cut short by the machine's terrible engine.

The combine door clanged open. "Maria!" Chester yelled into the darkness. "Maria!" He jumped down from the combine. "Maria, where are you?"

He ran back to where the combine had cut a swath in

the wheat with its straight header. "Maria! Wait a second, I see something. It's . . . it's her shoe. Oh, Maria . . .."

The sound of the combine faded into the distance.

§

"Whew!" Chad sat back in his chair after listening to the playback. "That's some pretty intense stuff. Nice work on the revisions, Joyce."

She smiled. "Thanks, but I did have a bit of help from my little brother." She ruffled Matt's hair.

"Don't forget dream boy over here," Matt said, pulling away from her and nudging Dean. "Nice performance, by all of you, and great work with the sound effects, Andrew and Chad."

Andrew grinned. "Thanks."

"So, I guess that's a wrap." Matt stood up and stretched. "Now all we have to do is get the tape to the swamp and—"

"Marsh," Dean interjected.

"Whatever. As I was saying, all we have to do is get episode two to the marsh, and we're home free."

"Okay, but can someone else distract Ms. Blunt this time?" Dean asked. "Last week, she gave me a tape with ten bird calls to memorize, and I haven't even memorized one of them yet. I'm scared enough of her when she's happy. I don't want to know what she looks like when she gets angry."

"Who's Ms. Blunt?" Joyce asked.

Matt looked at her in surprise. "You haven't met Henrietta yet?"

Joyce shook her head.

Matt grinned at the other boys. "I think we just found our distraction."

"Forget it," Joyce said, standing up to stretch. "I already saved your bacon by fixing your script. You can do your own dirty work."

"Fair enough," Matt said, looking at Dean. "We have other ways of distracting her."

Dean held up his hands in protest—and winced. "I don't know what you're thinking, but you can forget it!"

13

A LATE-NIGHT DISCOVERY

Ten minutes before midnight that Saturday, across the town of Milligan Creek and throughout the surrounding area, young hands turned on radios, tuning in to the Wetlands Unlimited frequency. Some snuck down into their basement rec room to listen. Others hid under the blankets in their bedroom, flashlights creating a glowing tent. Still others gathered in small listening parties, too afraid to face the next episode on their own.

Meanwhile, a mild breeze rustled the bulrushes along the edge of the Milligan Creek Heritage Marsh, the pockets of black water glinting under a full moon. The only other sounds came from a few frogs and waterfowl settling in for the night—and the guy-wires on the radio tower humming in the wind.

Inside the interpretive center, a single light burned in the window. It came from the lamp on Henrietta's desk, an ancient gray gooseneck lamp she had inherited from her grandfather. Considering her job and her passion for waterfowl, it couldn't have been more appropriate. Wearing oversized headphones, she was just finishing her recording of the following week's broadcast.

"Bobolink. That word is fun to say, isn't it? Bobolink, bobolink, bobolink. Give it a try sometime. But nothing matches the thrill of seeing one perched on a branch or a swaying bulrush and listening to it chirp away. 'A mad, reckless song fantasia, an outbreak of pent-up irrepressible glee.' That's how naturalist, bird lover, composer, and artist F. Schuyler Mathews described it. In case you've never heard one before, here's a brief sample of a male bobolink I recorded just this morning." She hit "play" on a tape player and smiled as it played the bird's bubbling, tinkling song.

A few moments later, she stopped the tape and leaned in close to the microphone. "That's just one of the top ten bird songs I have available for free for any young birdwatchers—or even old birdwatchers—who want to develop their wetlands IQ. Memorize them all, and you'll win a prize! I've already got at least one young birdwatcher out there working on it. Dean, if you're listening, don't leave me hanging! Well, that's all for this week, folks. Keep tuning in, and I'll keep tuning you up. This is Henrietta Blunt from Wetlands Unlimited keeping you sharp!"

She hit "stop" on the recording device and took off her headphones, smiling in satisfaction. "Not bad, if I say so myself. Hey, Woody?"

She scratched the head of a stuffed beaver her parents had given her as a gift when she first got her job with Wetlands Unlimited and then leaned back and stretched. She checked her watch. It was five minutes to midnight. It wasn't technically Sunday yet, but why wait until morning?

She hit a few buttons on the broadcast device, archived the previous week's recording, and then started broadcasting the new show. She turned on the speakers to make sure it was working as she prepared to head home for the night.

An introductory musical fanfare was followed by her voice. "Heeeeerrrre's Henrietta! Blunt, that is, resident

94

Wetlands Unlimited expert at your service. If you've never been to the Milligan Creek Heritage Marsh, I feel sorry for you! I really do, because you're missing out on one of the most spectacular attractions in the area! But you can fix that problem just by . . .."

§

Up in the tree house, Matt checked his watch anxiously as Chad turned on Henrietta's broadcast. "This is always the worst part," Matt said, "hoping nothing screws up."

"It won't screw up," Andrew said, sounding slightly offended. "I also made another slight modification."

"What's that?" Joyce asked. It was her first time up in the tree house and their first time listening to a broadcast with her, and her presence had all the guys on edge—especially Dean. He had insisted on spending an hour beforehand cleaning the tree house and airing it out. He had even climbed a ladder outside and washed the windows.

"I set it so that right after this episode ends, it plays episodes one and two back to back, just in case someone missed them last week."

"Good thinking," Matt said.

"Isn't that a little risky?" Dean asked. "It increases the amount of time we're on air, which increases our chances of getting caught."

"I wouldn't worry about it," Matt said. "Who except kids like us is even listening at this hour?"

§

Her eyes bleary from a long day at the marsh, Henrietta was just about to turn off the speakers when she was startled by a burst of static.

95

"What the heck?"

She went to the broadcast device to make sure everything was functioning normally. All the lights were in the green. Then her ears perked up as eerie music sounded on the speakers, followed by a voice. "Ladies and gentlemen, humankind is an intelligent species, a powerful species, an innovative and inventive species, able to plumb the ocean's depths and scan the far reaches of space . . .." She stared at the speakers, dumbstruck, as the voice continued. "But human beings are also proud creatures, prone to think too highly of themselves, to believe they are capable of anything . . ."

She jabbed buttons and turned knobs, but the voice continued. "But wherever the light of human knowledge shines, it can't help but create shadows, murky pockets of ignorance, mystery, and fear."

Finally, she popped out her tape, thinking that would be the end of it, but the voice kept going. "Within these shadows, hidden forces are at work in our world, dark forces, malevolent powers that will not be ignored."

"Okay, this is downright spooky," she said as the music shifted to a low bass rumble that made the lamp on Henrietta's desk vibrate, casting weird, distorted shadows on the wall and putting a menacing glint in Woody's eye.

"Every so often, these forces manifest themselves in a powerful way as a reminder, a warning, that we ignore them . . . at our—"

The voice was cut off as Henrietta turned off the speakers. She stared at them for a moment. Then she grabbed her coat and hat, turned off the lights, and ran out the door.

§

"What is this place?" Maria asked. "One minute I was running away from that combine, and now I'm stuck down in a—"

"Maria!" Chester's voice sounded muffled and faint as he cried her name in anguish.

"Chester? Chester! I'm down here!"

Chester leapt to his feet. "Maria? What? How—"

"Down here!"

"Her voice sounds muffled, as if it's coming from—"

"Chester! Down here! I fell into some kind of hole!"

"Keep talking!" Chester said as he walked through the grain. "I'll follow your voice. Are you hurt?"

"I don't think so. I don't know how, but one second I was running, thinking I was about to be killed by the combine, and the next thing I knew—"

"There you are! Thank goodness! Here, I'll kneel down. Can you reach my hand? Wait a second, I think I've got a—"

"Flashlight!" Maria said. "Perfect. Shine it around in here."

"Wow," Chester said a moment later. "It looks like an old cellar."

"What's it doing out here in the middle of the field?" Maria asked.

"I don't know. Here, take the flashlight while I—"

"No, don't! Then we'll both be trapped down here."

"I don't think so." Chester grunted as he lowered himself down. "There's a table over there in the corner. We should be able to stand on that and climb out."

Chester dropped down and then stood up and dusted himself off. "Can I see that flashlight again? Hmm . . . There's not much down here. Just a chair and a table, a couple of old jars, and—"

"A book!" Maria said. "Come closer with the light."

The sound of shuffling feet was followed by someone turning pages.

"It looks like an old journal," Maria said. "And look here. The last few pages have been torn out."

Just then, they heard the rumble of the combine. Dirt sprinkled down from the ceiling.

"We should get out of here," Chester said. "Get back to the house before it returns."

"Chester, who's driving it? Who's trying to kill us?"

Chester let out a long sigh. "I don't know how to tell you this, Maria, but when I climbed onto the combine and whipped open the door, ready to punch the lights out of whoever was in there, the cab was . . . empty."

"What?"

§

Listening to the end of the broadcast in her truck, Henrietta turned off the radio and sat back in shock—and then anger. Someone was interfering with her broadcast, her precious Wetlands Unlimited radio broadcast, and she was going to find out who—and make them pay.

14

"I WANT TO REPORT A HIJACKING."

"Get the second episode here! That's right, one episode for two dollars, two episodes for three! Available for a limited time only. Get them while supplies last!"

Like the previous week, a line-up of kids formed quickly by Darryl's locker, crumpled bills exchanged for cassette tapes, which had been upgraded to include hand-drawn inserts that featured the show's title and a drawing of a combine bearing down on two hapless victims.

"What have we here?" a voice asked, bringing all buying and selling to a halt.

The students turned as Mr. Karky, a stocky, grim-faced man, stepped forward. He was their gym teacher and football coach, and he was as strict as they came.

"Hand it over, McPherson." Mr. Karky held out his hand to Darryl, who reluctantly surrendered a sample of his merchandise.

Mr. Karky squinted at the cassette. "'It Came . . . from the Grain'? What's this, a tutorial on farming?"

"Not exactly, sir, it's—"

"What have you been told about conducting commerce on school property?" Mr. Karky tapped the cassette on the palm of his hand, his eyes boring into Darryl.

Darryl hung his head. "Not to do it."

"Exactly. And you were doing it because . . .."

"Look at the demand, sir." Darryl gestured at the crowd. "I couldn't resist the opportunity."

Mr. Karky eyeballed the students. None of them had the courage to meet his gaze. "I should confiscate all your tapes and your money and put it toward my retirement fund. But the Roughriders won last night, so I'm feeling especially generous this morning. So, all of you, get lost."

The students quickly dispersed, relieved at having gotten off easily.

"As for you, McPherson," Mr. Karky turned back to him and held up the cassette, "I'm holding onto this. And if there's anything inappropriate on here—"

"Definitely not, sir."

"—you're going to have far bigger problems than me on your hands."

Darryl swallowed hard and nodded as Mr. Karky strolled off toward the staff room.

Down the hall, Matt, Chad, Andrew, and Dean exchanged a worried look, having witnessed the exchange.

"Should we say something to him?" Chad asked.

"To who," Matt replied. "Karky?"

"No, Darryl."

"Like what, you owe us a ten percent royalty on every tape?" Matt shook his head. "Just keep your mouth shut and your head down. That goes for all of you. Got it?"

The other boys nodded silently.

"Moo."

They all turned to find Ben standing behind them. He was great at sneaking up on people.

"Hi, Ben," Matt said, hoping he hadn't overheard their conversation.

"There's still no cows in the program."

"Yeah, I noticed that," Matt said. "Maybe it'll change with the next episode."

Ben pouted. "I hope so."

§

At the Milligan Creek RCMP detachment, Staff Sergeant Romanowski was filling out a report at his desk when his intercom buzzed.

"Yes, what is it, Ruth?" he asked, addressing the detachment's receptionist, Mrs. Ruth Halushka.

"Someone to see you here, sir. A Ms. Blunt."

Romanowski frowned at the intercom. "Blunt?"

"Henrietta Blunt," Henrietta said, barging into his office. "And we have a problem."

Mrs. Halushka, a middle-aged woman prone to wearing long, floral-printed skirts, even during the winter, hurried in after her. "I'm sorry, Sergeant Romanowski, I tried to—"

"It's okay, Ruth." Romanowski set his report aside as Ruth retreated from his office, closing the door behind her. "What can I do for you, Ms. Blunt?"

"I'm sorry for being so . . . blunt," she reached forward to shake his hand, "but it comes with the name. I'm relatively new in town and, as you can see," she tapped the crest on the breast pocket of her shirt, "I'm with Wetlands Unlimited. You may have heard, but we have our own radio station, broadcasting twenty-four hours a day."

Romanowski nodded. "Yes, I've heard it. I knew I recognized your lovely voice."

Henrietta blushed slightly, unused to such compliments. "Yes, well, I do take pride in my work. At any rate, I'm here to report a serious crime that happened at midnight last Sunday morning."

Romanowski pursed his lips, his forehead furrowed. "A crime? What sort of crime?"

"A hijacking."

"A hijacking?"

"Yes. Perpetuated by terrorists."

"Terrorists? At the marsh?"

"No, in the air."

Romanowski pushed his chair back from his desk and frowned. "I'm sorry, but I don't think I understand."

"This past Sunday, at precisely twelve o'clock a.m., someone hijacked my radio signal."

"Really? How?"

"That's what I'm here to find out."

"What did they broadcast?"

"Some kind of . . . radio drama. It was actually quite good—not to mention scary. I listened to both episodes, and I had to keep a night light on afterwards, so I could sleep. But that's beside the point. It has no place on my station, and I want you to find out who did it and shut them down."

Romanowski nodded slowly as he processed the news. "Are you sure it's someone local? I mean, I remember one night I was scrolling through the dial, and I was able to pick up stations from as far away as Florida. Maybe it's just some kind of atmospheric interference."

Henrietta took a deep breath. "I don't want to insult your intelligence, sir, but that phenomenon, known as a skywave or a skip, where radio waves reflect back toward Earth off the ionosphere, is only possible with low-frequency AM or shortwave signals. My radio station broadcasts in FM, and it only has about a thirty-five-kilometer radius, so, the perpetrators have to be somewhere right in this area."

Romanowski wiggled his mustache, a habit when he was deep in thought. Then he stood up and reached for his hat and jacket, which hung on a coat rack in the corner. "It's about time I paid a visit to the marsh. What'd you say your first name was again, ma'am?"

"Henrietta. Henrietta Blunt."

Romanowski smiled. "Henrietta. How could I forget a pretty name like that?"

Unable to restrain a giddy grin, Henrietta's face turned as crimson as the feathers on a red-winged blackbird.

§

Right after lunch, Matt, Andrew, and Dean settled in to English class, along with the rest of their classmates. Chad was a grade ahead of them, so he was in the physics lab.

"Good morning, students," said their teacher, Mr. Priebe, his bald head shining as he hurried in the door at the back of the classroom. "Sorry I'm late, but I was just listening to a fascinating recording Mr. Karky played for the teachers in the staff room."

Dean, Matt, and Andrew exchanged a look.

"Courtesy Darryl McPherson, apparently," Mr. Priebe continued.

Darryl smiled and waved.

Dean's hand shot up. "Actually, he's just recording the show off the radio. Someone else is broadcasting it."

Matt and Andrew scowled at him, with Matt mouthing the words "Shut up!" through clenched teeth.

"Oh, and do you happen to know who is broadcasting it?" Mr. Priebe asked, his eyes probing Dean's worried face.

"Uh, no, I just . . . that's just what I heard. Darryl probably knows though."

All eyes turned to the young entrepreneur.

"I recorded it off the Wetlands Unlimited radio station last Saturday at midnight," Darryl said, "and the Saturday before that."

"Why would Wetlands Unlimited be broadcasting a radio drama?" Mr. Priebe asked.

Matt held up his hand. "Maybe they're just trying to get listeners hooked on the station, so they'll tune in during the day and learn about ducks."

"Highly unlikely," Mr. Priebe replied. "At any rate, that's not what I wanted to talk about this afternoon. The show gave me an idea. Why don't we try writing our own radio drama and recording it together as a class?"

Ben raised his hand.

"Yes, Ben?"

"Can there be cows in the show?"

Mr. Priebe thought about it for a moment. "I don't see why not."

"I have an idea for a show," Dean said, glancing at Matt, who scowled at him again. "It's about these little people who are born when the grain is planted, but they can't leave the field, and they only live until the grain is harvested. Then one day they see a kid walking along and think he's a little person, just like them, so they decide to lure him into the field to see what makes him different. They think if they're able to leave the grain field, they'll be able to live longer than just one season. But once they realize the kid is just a kid and not a little person like them, they decide to hold him hostage and lure other kids into the field so they can stop the farmer from harvesting the grain, and they won't disappear."

"Interesting," Mr. Priebe said, nodding slowly. "In fact, that's an excellent idea."

Dean beamed in satisfaction, until he saw Ben glowering at him. "Oh, and there's also this cow in the story," Dean added. "A magical cow. It's what saves the kids in the end."

Ben's smile could be seen from a mile away.

§

"I'm sorry, Henrietta, but I don't see anything unusual around this radio tower," Staff Sergeant Romanowski said, resting his hand on a guy-wire.

"What about at the top?"

Romanowski craned his head up, squinting in the sun. "Could I borrow your binoculars for a moment?"

She handed them to him, and he used them to examine the top of the tower. "Nothing unusual up there either. Except for that owl."

"I put it there," Henrietta confessed. "To keep the woodpeckers away. See how its head bobbles when the wind blows? It almost looks real."

Romanowski lowered the binoculars and looked at her. "Woodpeckers?"

"Yes. Turns out they're trying to bore holes into my observation tower. I have an owl on there as well."

Romanowski continued staring at her for a moment and then shook his head as if to clear it. "Anyway, whoever's hijacking your signal would need a power source and a fairly large device. If it was up there, we'd see it."

"What about inside the interpretive center? Are you sure you looked everywhere?"

"Yep. Didn't find anything out of the ordinary in there either." Romanowski wiggled his mustache and then held up his index finger. "You know, that gives me an idea. Maybe there's nothing hidden around here. Maybe whoever's doing it is sneaking in at night with the equipment, broadcasting the show, and then sneaking out again as soon as it's done."

Henrietta tensed with indignation. "Are you talking about trespassing? On Wetlands Unlimited property?"

"Well, technically, the property belongs to the province; Wetlands Unlimited just manages it, but, yes."

Henrietta paused to think for a moment. "But I was here the other night when they did it."

"Yes, but you weren't looking for them. They could have been here the entire time."

"That's it!" Henrietta's eyes ignited with passion. "A stakeout! I'll hide out in a duck blind this Saturday night and catch the terrorists in the act!"

"Well, they may be hijacking your signal, but that doesn't exactly make them terrorists. Technically speaking, terrorists are—"

"The show is scary, is it not?"

"Yes, but—"

"Then, technically, they are using my radio station to terrorize the community. Do you disagree?"

"No, but—"

"Then they are terrorists, and they must be stopped."

Romanowski sighed. "If you say so."

Both fell silent for a moment. Then Romanowski looked up. "Say, there wouldn't be room for two in that duck blind, would there?"

For the third time that day, Henrietta blushed.

15

THE HEAT IS ON

The following Saturday morning, Dean snatched a leftover waffle off the counter, squirted a dollop of syrup on it, and was nearly out the door when his mother's voice stopped him cold in his tracks.

"And where do you think you're going?"

Dean turned to face her, the waffle in his mouth. He tore off a bite, chewed it quickly, and then swallowed, buying himself a moment to think. "To the, uh, to the marsh. You know, doing my usual Saturday thing."

Mrs. Muller crossed her arms. "I don't like how that woman has you working for her all the time—for free, no less. If you're that bored, I have plenty of chores for you to do at home."

"I'm not bored," Dean replied. "I just really like it out there."

Mrs. Muller frowned. "Since when have you cared so much about ducks?"

"It's not just ducks, Mom. It's geese, swans, garganeys, brandts, scaups, scoters, loons, bobolinks, plovers, coots, wigeons—"

"Don't you mean 'pigeons'? And what the heck is a bobolink?"

"No, I mean 'wigeons.' It's a duck with a dark brown head and a pinky-brown chest. And a bobolink is—"

"I don't care what a bobolink is. I care that my son is never around anymore on Saturdays. Have you seen how high the grass is?"

"I'll cut it tomorrow."

"Tomorrow's Sunday. That's our family day."

"I'll cut it tonight then."

Mrs. Muller pursed her lips.

"Seriously. I'm sorry I've been gone so much," Dean said. "I thought you and Dad would be excited about me volunteering out there. I'm learning a lot. The other day, I even saw a king elder and—"

"That all sounds fine and dandy, but something still doesn't add up. Does Matt Taylor have anything to do with your visits out there?"

Dean, who had taken another bite of waffle, nearly choked as he attempted to force it down. "Sometimes," he said, pounding his chest.

"Oh really," Mrs. Muller replied, circling in for the kill. "And what exactly does *he* do out there?"

Dean shrugged, unable to keep his face from reddening. "Oh, you know, stuff."

"What kind of 'stuff'?"

"You know, maintenance stuff. Painting. Fixing."

Mrs. Muller scoffed in disbelief. "I've never seen Matt Taylor fix anything."

Dean took another bite of waffle, chewing silently as he struggled to come up with something to say.

Finally, his mother heaved a huge sigh. "Well, I'll let you go today, but you better get home in time to cut that grass. And if I find out you've been up to something else . . .."

"Don't worry, Mom," Dean said, already halfway out the door. "I'll have that lawn in tip-top shape before supper!"

Mrs. Muller stepped up to the screen door and watched Dean wheel his bike out of the garage and then peddle away. When she turned away from the door, she noticed something hanging on the coat rack: Dean's bike helmet. She grabbed it and flung open the screen door. "Dean, you forgot your—" But he was already out of sight.

As she hung his helmet back on his hook, she saw his school backpack sitting on the floor beneath it. She put her hands on her hips and sighed. "How many times do I have to tell that boy to hang up his backpack when he gets home from school?"

Shaking her head, she grabbed his backpack and hung it on his hook. As she did, a paper floated out of it. She snatched it off the floor and was about to stick it back into his pack when she paused to read it. "Radio show ideas?" She read a bit more. "Little people hidden in the grain? A magical cow?" She arched her eyebrow and shook her head. "Weird."

She folded the paper and stuck it back into Dean's backpack. Then she paused and looked in the direction Dean had just gone.

§

By the time Dean reached the marsh, the other boys were all waiting for him.

"What took you so long?" Matt asked.

"My mom," Dean said between breaths, winded after the long ride. "She was asking me all sorts of questions about why I keep coming here. I think she's getting suspicious."

"What did you tell her?" Chad asked, sweeping his hair out of his eyes as he frowned in concern.

"Just a bunch of stuff about all the birds I see here. She also asked about you, Matt."

Matt rolled his eyes. "Of course."

"If anyone asks, you do a lot of painting and fixing out here."

Chad laughed. "Matt fix things? All I've ever seen him do is destroy things. Not that the rest of us are much better. Except for you, Andrew."

Dean smirked. "That's what my mom said—about Matt, I mean."

"Very funny," Matt said. "Anyway—hey, what's duck lady doing?"

The group looked over to see Henrietta carrying a rucksack to the edge of the bulrushes. She set it on the ground, unzipped it, and pulled out poles and what looked like a tent.

"We'll go check it out," Chad said, starting toward her. "Might be a good chance for you and Andrew to do your thing. Come on, Dean."

"Can't I just wait here?" Dean asked. "I still haven't memorized all those bird calls yet, and I have to get back in time to cut the grass before supper."

"Don't worry about it," Chad said. "Looks like she has something other than bird calls on her mind."

A moment later, the two boys approached Henrietta, who was examining a set of instructions. She looked up as they approached. "A-ha! Good morning! You're just in time . . . to help me bust a crime."

"Uh, don't you mean 'bust a rhyme'?" Chad asked.

"No!" Henrietta's nostrils flared. "I mean a crime, and a serious one too."

"What kind of crime?" Dean glanced nervously toward the interpretive center, behind which Andrew and Matt had just disappeared.

"Hijacking!"

Dean swallowed hard as he looked at Chad. "Hijacking? In a duck marsh?"

"Yes! A hijacking incident has taken place right here under my nose, and I'm going to use this," she nudged the equipment at her feet, "to catch the culprits."

Chad looked down at the ground. "You're going to catch them in a tent?"

"This is no tent." Henrietta grabbed the material, which was printed with images of bulrushes as camouflage. "This is a duck blind. We're going to hide in it tonight, and when those terrorists show up to broadcast their little show, we'll be waiting to catch them."

"We?" Dean instinctively took a step back. "I'm sorry, but I don't think my mother—"

He was interrupted by a car horn honking at the marsh entrance. All three of them looked toward the sound. Dean's mouth fell open in shock. "My mother!"

"Visitors!" Henrietta dropped the instructions and started toward the vehicle. "We'll deal with the duck blind later."

"Wait!" Dean hurried after her. "Like I said, we can't come here and sit in a duck blind all night and—"

Henrietta stopped and smiled at him. "I'm sorry. When I said 'we,' I didn't mean you guys—as great as it would be to introduce you all to what this wonderful prairie pothole ecosystem sounds like at night."

Dean's shoulders sagged in relief. "Oh, good."

"By 'we,' I meant to say Staff Sergeant Romanowski is will accompany me."

Dean's eyebrows shot up. "The police officer?"

"Yes!" She pointed her index finger at him. "But don't get any funny ideas. It's not a date—no matter what Staff Sergeant Romanowski might think. It's strictly business!"

With that, she hurried off toward Mrs. Muller, who was just getting out of her car. "Hello! Welcome to the

Milligan Creek Heritage Marsh!"

As soon as she was gone, Chad chuckled. "Staff Sergeant Romanowski has the hots for Henrietta Blunt? Who'd have thought?"

"Forget about that!" Dean said. "He's a police officer. Did you hear that? We're going to get busted by the RCMP."

"No, we're not. You heard her. She has no idea how we're doing it. They can sit in that duck blind all night if they want. It won't change a thing. We sneak the tapes in during the day and—oh no, Matt and Andrew!"

Moments later, Dean and Chad jogged up to Mrs. Muller's car, breathing heavily.

"Why, Dean," Henrietta said, turning toward him, "you didn't tell me your mother was coming out here today."

Dean gave his mother a furtive look. "That's because I didn't know she was coming out here. Hi, Mom."

"Hello, Dean," Mrs. Muller said, her voice betraying no hint of her earlier suspicion. "Ms. Blunt here—"

"Please, call me Henrietta," Ms. Blunt said, smiling.

An uncomfortable smile settled over Mrs. Muller's lips. "Uh, if it's okay with you, Ms. Blunt, I prefer Dean not to call adults by their first name."

"No problem, ma'am," Henrietta said, giving a mock salute. "Ms. Blunt it is. Got that, *Mr.* Muller?" Dean jumped as she nudged him in the ribs.

"Anyway," Mrs. Muller said, not at all pleased with Henrietta's joke, "Ms. Blunt here was just telling us about all the great work you've been doing out here."

"That's right." Henrietta put her arm around Dean's shoulders. "If he keeps it up, one day it'll be him wearing this fine uniform and running this place. Isn't that right, Dean?"

"Uh, yeah." He backed out from under her arm as politely as possible.

Mrs. Muller looked around curiously. "Where are the other boys?"

Henrietta's eyebrows knit together. "Boys? Which other boys?"

At that moment, Matt and Andrew stepped out from behind the interpretive center—and froze.

"Those boys," Mrs. Muller said, spotting them immediately, as only a suspicious mother could. "Hello, Andrew," she said, all but tenting her fingers in diabolical delight. "Hello, *Matt*."

16

The Stakeout

"That's strange," Henrietta said, "I had no idea anyone else was here."

"Oh really," Mrs. Muller said, casting a sideways glare at Dean, who swallowed hard.

"Uh, that's my brother," Chad said, his mind scrambling. "Matt, that is. You remember the other one, Henri—I mean, Ms. Blunt. It's Andrew. You gave him a sticker during our school field trip."

Henrietta smacked herself in the forehead. "How could I forget!" She turned to Mrs. Muller. "That boy is a budding naturalist if I've ever seen one. Brilliant mind on him."

"What about the other boy?" Mrs. Muller asked. "The scruffy-haired one with the ball cap?"

Henrietta studied Matt for a moment as the boys approached and then shook her head. "Don't know if I've ever seen him."

"Interesting," Mrs. Muller said, her eyes boring holes into her son.

"Hello, Henrietta, Mrs. Muller," Matt said cheerily as he and Andrew walked up. "What a beautiful day to be in the marsh!"

"Hello, boys," Henrietta said. "What are you up to back there? I didn't see you come in."

"Uh, I have a bit of an experiment running," Andrew said, "checking the pH balance of the water at various places in the marsh." He held up a vial of murky water as evidence. "I'm going to be away on vacation for a couple of weeks this summer, so I was just showing Matt how to take the measurements when I'm gone."

"pH balance?" Mrs. Muller scoffed. "A likely story. I bet Matt doesn't even know what those letters stand for."

"Actually, pH stands for powers of hydrogen," Matt said, "which is a measurement of the hydrogen ion concentration in a body of water. The scale ranges from one to fourteen, with seven considered neutral and anything below that acidic and anything above that alkaline or basic."

Mrs. Muller stared at him, dumbfounded.

"That, my boy, deserves a sticker!" Henrietta dug one out of her fanny pack, peeled off the backing, and stuck it to Matt's chest. "As for you," she turned to Andrew, "why didn't you tell me you were running an experiment in the marsh? I could have helped you."

"I wanted to surprise you with the results. The good news is, so far, the water's right where it should be, between six and eight, which is typical for a prairie pothole ecosystem like this."

If Henrietta could have smiled any wider, her face probably would have split in half. "Prairie pothole ecosystem—he even got the terminology right. Would it be alright if I—" Without waiting for a response, she gripped him in a side hug. "No offense to my *numero uno* birdwatcher here," she said, indicating Dean, "but this really takes the cake."

Andrew offered a tight-lipped smile, his body rigid.

Mrs. Muller crossed her arms, unconvinced. "It takes

the cake, all right."

Henrietta released Andrew, to his relief, and turned to Mrs. Muller. "Well, Audrey—or would you prefer me to call you Mrs. Muller?" She winked at the boys. "Let me give you a quick tour of the place, and then you can go wandering off on your own."

Mrs. Muller held up her hands in protest. "That's okay, I only came here to—"

"Don't worry, it'll only take a few minutes. Just a quick orientation, and you'll be off to the races." Henrietta put her hand on Mrs. Muller's shoulder and gave her a gentle push toward the interpretive center.

"Oh, but I really must—well, okay, I guess a few minutes wouldn't hurt."

As the two women walked away, Dean stared at them in amazement. "I can't believe it, someone who can actually out-muscle my mom."

"Smooth move with the pH balance lecture, professor," Chad said to his brother. "Where'd you come up with all that?"

Matt pointed at Andrew. "He gave me a quick briefing on the way over here."

"Where'd you get the vial of water?" Dean asked.

"That's the best part," Matt said. "We weren't lying. He really is running an experiment!"

The other boys laughed as Andrew reddened. "What's wrong with that?" he asked. "I started to get a little concerned when she talked about agricultural run-off during our field trip."

"There's nothing wrong with it," Chad said. "I just wonder what else is going on in that incredible mind of yours. Did you guys get the tape set up at least?"

"Of course," Matt said.

"Wait a second." Dean's face flushed as he suddenly

remembered what Henrietta had told them earlier about the duck blind and Staff Sergeant Romanowski. "We've got way bigger problems."

§

Henrietta pulled her striped wool Hudson's Bay blanket closer, shivering despite the numerous layers she was wearing. She checked her watch. "Ten minutes to midnight, and still no sign of them." She peered out one of the slits in the duck blind.

"Here, this oughta help." Romanowski held out a steaming enamel mug. "Coffee—with a little something extra." He winked.

"Thanks." She took the mug from him. "The cool, damp air really settles in here at night."

"Tell me about it." The staff sergeant rubbed his gloved hands together.

"Whew!" Henrietta grimaced as she sipped her drink. "You really did put something extra in there. What is it?"

Romanowski put his right fist to his chest and grinned. "Trade secret. A little concoction we created back during cadet training to get us through the long, cold winter in Regina."

Henrietta pulled out a transistor radio and turned it on, her canned voice suddenly blaring in the duck blind. "Loons are a rare sight in this part of the province, but every so often—"

She turned the volume down. "Sorry!" She peered out the slit. "I hope that didn't spook them!"

Romanowski also looked out. "I don't think so. I don't hear anything anyway."

Suddenly, Henrietta realized their faces were almost

touching. She pulled back. "I feel so helpless in here, like we should be out there patrolling or something."

"Trust me," Romanowski said, his mustache wiggling as he took a sip from his mug. "I've been on plenty of stakeouts. All we need is patience. There's no need to go chasing after the perpetrators. We have the upper hand. They're going to come straight to us."

§

Matt hugged his pillow as he lay on his stomach on one of the top bunks in the tree house. "Man, I don't know what's better, this episode or knowing that, right now, Henrietta Blunt and Staff Sergeant Romanowski are freezing their butts off in the marsh trying to catch a bunch of 'terrorists' who will never show up."

"Well, I don't like it," Dean said. "We're getting too cocky, and that always leads to trouble. We got lucky today, but I know my mom still suspects something."

"She can suspect all she wants," Matt replied. "All that matters is what she can prove." He checked his watch. "Now be quiet. It's about to start."

He reached over and turned up the volume.

§

Pages rustled as someone flipped through them.

"This journal is incredible," Maria said. "It's like someone kept a record of everyone in town."

"But why?" Chester asked. "It's like they were some kind of spy. And look at this, a map of the village, but what are those things?"

"Black lines running from building to building," Maria said. "Pipes, maybe? Power lines?"

119

"This book looks way too old for either of those," Chester replied.

"Wait a second," Maria said. "I've got it . . . tunnels!"

"Really?" Chester asked. "Why would all the buildings in a small prairie village be connected by tunnels?"

"I don't know," Maria replied, "but I know how we can find out."

"Oh yeah, how's that?"

"Go back to that creepy basement in the middle of the grain field."

"But the combine is still out there—and who knows what else."

"I know," Maria said, "but if the tunnels are real, that won't matter."

"What do you mean?"

Footsteps sounded as Maria walked away.

"Hey, where are you going?"

"The basement, dummy." Maria flicked a light switch.

"But what do you—of course!"

Their feet pounded down the stairs.

§

"They've got to be here somewhere!" Henrietta said, running down the boardwalk, flashlight in hand. Romanowski was right behind her. Both stopped and swept their flashlights across the marsh. All they saw was bulrushes, grass, and patches of dark water. A few startled waterfowl murmured in the distance.

"To the radio tower!" Henrietta cried, already running toward it.

§

"Do you really think there could be a tunnel in the basement of our house?" Chester asked over the sound of boxes and other items being moved.

"Why not?" Maria replied. "If this house is as old as you say, then that would make it one of the originals. And if we can figure out which one it is, we can figure out where it is on the map."

"Wait a second," Chester said. "Do you mean to say an entire village once stood where our farm is now?"

"If this journal is accurate, then yes, and seeing as we found it in an old basement that had been covered up in the middle of a field, I'd say it is. Now help me move these boxes away from the wall."

§

"No one back here!" Henrietta shouted as she ran out from behind the interpretive center.

"Nothing out of the ordinary here either," Romanowski replied, shining his flashlight up the tower.

"Strange . . .." Henrietta turned slowly in a circle and shone her flashlight out at the marsh while she held the radio to her ear. "Could they be sitting in a canoe somewhere? Why didn't I think to bring one?"

§

Tink, tink, tink.
"Nothing so far," Chester said.

"Keep tapping," Maria replied. "There's got to be an opening somewhere."

Tink, tink, tonk.

121

"What was that?" Maria asked.

Tonk, tonk.

"That's it!" she cried. "A hollow space behind the wall. Now what?"

"Let me get a sledgehammer from the machine shed," Chester said.

"Wait a second. It's not safe out there. And besides, I don't want to be left down here alone."

"I'll be quick," Chester replied. "You can wait for me in the kitchen. Watch me out the window. You'll be able to see me the entire time."

"Except when you're in the machine shed."

Just then, the house creaked ominously. "That's it," Maria said. "I'm coming with you."

§

"Maybe they're broadcasting from a distance," Romanowski suggested, his eyes straining to see in the darkness. "Using some kind of remote transmitter. But that would take an enormous amount of power. And if they have that, it would make more sense to set up their own radio station than hijack yours."

"Unless they're purposefully trying to sabotage my station!" Henrietta said. "Wetlands Unlimited has some powerful enemies, you know."

"Like who?" Romanowski asked.

"Farmers."

"Farmers aren't powerful."

"Ever seen a bunch of them gathered together in a room protesting something? Talk about scary."

"Even so, why would they hate Wetlands Unlimited?"

"We keep asking them to stop draining their sloughs so we can preserve waterfowl habitat."

"Well, even if farmers were behind the show, I don't think they'd start their broadcast at midnight, and they certainly wouldn't be broadcasting a radio drama about a haunted farm. It makes farmers look like the bad guys."

"Good point," Henrietta admitted.

She and Romanowski were silent for a moment, deep in thought, her frowning and him wiggling his mustache. Then her face lit up. "That leaves us with only one option."

"What's that?" Romanowski asked, following her as she marched toward the interpretive center.

"They've been right under our noses all along."

"But we've already searched for a transmitter," Romanowski said. "We didn't find anything."

Henrietta whipped open the interpretive center's door. "Time to look harder."

Romanowski looked at his watch, sighed, and then followed her inside.

17

FRONT-PAGE NEWS

Hours later, Staff Sergeant Romanowski flopped into a chair in Henrietta's office, exhausted. He checked his watch and then rubbed his eyes, which were red and glassy from lack of sleep. "It's two thirty in the morning, Henrietta. Don't you think it's time we called it a night?"

Henrietta set down a case of birdwatching books she had opened to see if anything was hidden inside and then sat on the corner of her desk. "I guess you're right. I'm just mystified about how they're doing it."

"I am too," Romanowski admitted, standing up. "Maybe we'll be able to think clearer after we've had some sleep. I'll be sure to call you if I come up with anything."

"Thank you, Richard," Henrietta said. "I really appreciate your help on this."

"All in the name of duty, ma'am." Romanowski took off his cap and bowed theatrically. "You know, you would have made a good police officer. You still could."

"And leave the marsh unprotected? Never!"

He smiled at her enthusiasm. "Goodnight—I mean, good morning. Whatever it is."

"Tell me about it," she said, yawning. "I have to be back here again to open in just over six hours."

"I'm sure no one would mind if you took the morning off. You've earned it."

"The marsh never sleeps, and neither do I," Henrietta replied, putting her fist to her chest.

Romanowski grinned. "If you say so. See ya."

"Goodbye, Richard."

She smiled as she closed the door behind him. Then she stretched and began to tidy a few things that had been dislodged in their search.

A few minutes later, on the way to her truck, Henrietta checked the doors on the public washrooms behind the interpretive center to ensure they were locked. As she checked the men's room, she heard a strange sound inside—water running.

She unlocked the door and looked at the sinks. They were off. Then she turned to the two toilets. It sounded like the water in the left toilet was running.

She stepped in and jiggled the handle, but the water continued to run. She lifted the lid off the tank to see if something was amiss. Sure enough, the chain had caught on something inside the tank: a black hard-shell case.

"Hmm . . . what's this doing in here?"

She pulled it out and then set it on the counter by the sinks. Grabbing some paper towels from the dispenser, she dried it off. Then she popped the latches and opened it, revealing a tangle of wires and glowing lights. Her eyes went wide with surprise and then narrowed to match her victorious grin.

"I've got you!"

§

When Matt got to school on Monday morning, he expected the usual discussions about the previous Saturday's broadcast. As he reached his locker, the other students were talking, all right, but it wasn't about the latest episode of *It Came . . . from the Grain.*

"Do they have any idea who planted it there?" one student asked as she walked past.

"No, but the news report said the police are certain they'll figure it out soon," her friend replied.

"That's such a bummer. Just when they were about to broadcast their final episode. Now we'll never know the secret behind why that town disappeared."

"What are you girls talking about?" Matt asked, coming up behind them.

"Oh, hi, Matt." The first girl, Bonnie, stopped and smiled. "Haven't you heard? It was on the radio this morning. The police found out who was broadcasting that radio show."

Matt swallowed hard. "They did?"

"Well, they found the device they were using to do it anyway," her friend, Debbie, corrected. "We were just saying it's too bad. I wish they could've found it a week from now instead."

"Yeah."

His throat suddenly dry, Matt leaned back against the lockers as the girls continued down the hall. He looked up as Chad approached. He had arrived at school early for a spring training football workout. Andrew and Dean were right behind him.

"I take it you heard?" Chad asked, noting the expression on his brother's face.

Matt nodded sullenly. "Yeah, just now."

"It's all the guys could talk about during football practice," Chad said as he opened his locker and stuffed his gym clothes inside.

"We are so dead." Dean leaned back against the locker

beside Matt. "We might as well just confess now. Maybe they'll go easier on us."

"No way," Matt said. "As far as we know, all they have is the device. There's no way to link it to any of us. Right, Andrew?"

"Right."

"What about fingerprints?" Dean asked.

Andrew shook his head. "I wiped everything down, and I made sure to wear surgical gloves whenever I handled the Hijacker."

Chad sighed. "That's a relief."

"Not for me." Dean stood up and opened his locker. "I just know they're going to figure it out sooner or later. And when my mom—"

"Just relax," Matt assured him. "Like I said, they don't have anything on us yet, and if we all keep our mouths shut—"

"Moo."

Matt turned around to find Ben standing behind them. "Ben. How long have you been there?"

"Long enough."

"Long enough for what?" Matt asked suspiciously.

"Long enough to know you're not talking about cows."

"You know, you really shouldn't sneak up on people like that," Chad said. "Sometimes what people are talking about is private."

"Sorry." Ben looked down sheepishly. "Moo."

The boys watched him walk away.

"Think he heard anything?" Chad asked.

"It's hard to say," Matt replied. "But I don't think we need to worry about him. If it's not about cows, I don't think he cares. All the same, like I said, we just need to keep our mouths shut. All of us. Understand?"

The other guys nodded. Then Dean glanced up, and his face fell. "Uh oh."

Everyone turned to see what he was looking at.

Joyce.

"Gotta go," Dean said, once again none too eager to bask in her glorious presence.

"Me too," Andrew said, right behind him.

"Hey, guys, wait—" Matt stopped himself mid-sentence and sighed. He knew he and Chad would have to face their sister's wrath on their own.

§

"Don't blame us. No one forced you to do it," Matt said moments later as he, Joyce, and Chad held a hurried conference just inside the door of the women's change room. Joyce had dragged them in there, so they could talk in private. "And can we get out of here? It's making me nervous."

"Yeah," Chad agreed.

A girl pushed the door open to enter, but Joyce slammed it shut. "It's occupied," she said, locking it.

"For how long?" the girl's muffled voice asked from the other side.

"Until we're finished!"

Joyce turned back to face her brothers, her eyes blazing. "I was counting on you guys to keep this a secret. You told me you had it covered."

Matt held up his index finger. "Technically, Andrew told you that."

Joyce jabbed her own index finger into Matt's chest, using it to emphasize each word. "But you're the ringleader, so that makes you responsible."

"Ow!" Matt rubbed his chest.

"The question is," Joyce continued, giving him a final poke, "what are you going to do about it?"

"Nothing."

She stared at Matt in disbelief. "What?"

"Nothing," Matt repeated. "There's no way to trace it back to us, so we just keep our mouths shut and wait for it all to blow over."

"We're talking about Henrietta Blunt here," Joyce said. "You really think she's going to let things just blow over?"

"She has a point, Matt," Chad admitted.

Just then, the PA system crackled as someone prepared to make an announcement. "If I could have your attention, please," their principal, Mr. Gibson, said. "All staff and students, please assemble in the gymnasium for an impromptu assembly. We'd like to get going as quickly as possible to minimize interference with our regular class schedule, so please proceed to the gym immediately. Thank you."

The three siblings looked at each other. "This can't be good," Chad said, voicing what they were all thinking.

§

Minutes later, three hundred students, along with their teachers and support staff, were assembled in the gymnasium. The crowd was bubbling with muted conversations speculating about the reason for the assembly. Matt and Chad found Dean and Andrew and sat down on the floor with them. Joyce refused to be seen with her co-conspirators and went off to sit with her friends.

"Good morning, students," Mr. Gibson said, adjusting his glasses, which rested on the bridge of his bulbous nose, which rested just above his bristling mustache, which was the same color as the remaining strands of white and gray hair that clung to his scalp, swept to one side in a classic comb-over. "I'm sorry to interrupt your schedule, but an important issue has come to our attention, and we'd like your help in solving it. To give you more details, I've asked a special guest to address us this morning. Ms. Blunt, please step forward."

All four boys felt like a bucket of ice water had just exploded in their stomachs. Matt glanced over at Joyce, who looked like she felt the same. A friend nudged her and whispered something in her ear, grinning as she pointed at Henrietta, no doubt making fun of her Wetlands Unlimited uniform. Joyce nodded and did her best to smile.

Henrietta took the mic from Mr. Gibson. "Thank you, Principal Gibson. Good morning, students. I wish my first opportunity to address your school could be under better circumstances, to extol the beauty and wonder of our local wetlands ecosystem. Instead, I'm sorry to say I'm here not to educate you but to alert you to a crime in which all of you have been unwitting participants—victims, even. A crime not just against me or Wetlands Unlimited or the Milligan Creek Heritage Marsh but against the very ecosystem itself. In truth, a crime against our nurturer, our mentor, our provider and sustainer of life, Mother Earth."

18

THE USUAL SUSPECTS

"Man, did she have to lay it on so thick?" Matt asked hours later as he lay on his bunk in the tree house, hands clasped behind his head as he stared at the ceiling.

"I know. She made it sound like we're some kind of eco-terrorists," Chad said, leaning back in one of the bucket seats and spinning himself slowly back and forth with his foot. "All we did was interrupt her precious broadcast for thirty minutes at midnight on Saturday when no one was listening to it anyway."

"Except Ben," said Andrew, who was sitting in one of the other bucket seats.

"And her timing couldn't have been worse," Matt added. "Right before we were going to air our final episode. Now no one will know how the story ends."

Suddenly, the trapdoor popped open. "We're busted," Dean said before he was even halfway inside.

Matt sat up. "What do you mean?"

"This." Dean tossed a copy of the *Milligan Creek Review* on the table. On the front page was the headline, "Plug Pulled on Pirate Radio Station." Beneath it was a photo of Henrietta proudly holding the Hijacker.

"So what?" Matt laid back down, unimpressed. "We

already know she found it."

"Read the story." Dean snatched up the paper and pointed at it. "After the assembly today, the janitor came forward and said he found the bundle of advertising slips I left behind when we had to escape from the school." Dean squinted at the paper as he read from it. "'This almost certainly points to student involvement, Staff Sergeant Romanowski said. Mr. Gibson, principal of MCCS, promised to do everything in his power to find the culprits.'" Dean lowered the paper, his face almost as white as the newsprint. "See what I mean? Busted." He threw the paper back onto the table.

The other boys fell silent as they processed the news. Then Matt slid down from his bunk. "This doesn't change anything. There's still nothing to link those slips of paper to us."

"Fingerprints?" Chad turned to Andrew, who shook his head.

"Not on paper."

"What about Romanowski seeing us hanging around the school that day?" Dean asked.

"He'll never put two and two together," Matt said. "Besides, they need proof. Suspicion isn't enough."

"But what if they question us?" Dean pressed. "There's no way I can lie to a police officer. Or Mr. Gibson. Not to mention Henrietta."

"There's no reason to question us," Matt said. "We're her favorite birdwatchers, remember? We just need to stay calm and see what happens next."

§

At school the following day, the atmosphere was decidedly muted. With the finger of blame potentially pointed at a member, or members, of the student body, everyone was a suspect, and everyone seemed to regard each other with suspicion.

As the boys walked past the principal's office on the way to their lockers, they saw Darryl sitting on the bench outside, the spot reserved for students who had run afoul of the school's disciplinary process. He had his head buried in the previous day's stock market news.

"Hey, Darryl, what's going on?" Matt asked.

Darryl looked up from his newspaper. "I don't know. My parents got a call last night from Mr. Gibson saying he wanted to talk to me as soon as I got to school this morning. Probably something to do with that radio thing. They probably think that because I was selling the tapes, I was behind it."

"Were you?" Matt asked, giving his buddies a knowing glance, proud of his quick thinking to steer the blame away from them.

"I wish I could take credit for it. But no, I was just taking advantage of a sales opportunity."

"Well, good luck in there."

"Thanks," Darryl replied, turning back to his stock market news.

The boys reconvened at their lockers, looking around nervously to ensure no one was listening to them. "Do you think they'll call in other students?" Dean asked.

"Maybe a few," Matt said. "Darryl made himself a target. But none of us have—"

"Andrew Loewen," the secretary's voice said over the intercom. "Could you please come to the principal's office? Andrew Loewen."

Matt, Chad, and Dean all looked at Andrew, whose face had suddenly turned bright red.

"Breathe, Andrew, breathe," Matt said, putting his

hand on his friend's shoulder. "Think of how cool you were under pressure with Ms. Blunt. This is no different. Don't lie, but don't answer their questions outright either. Find a way to answer without answering. Got it?"

Andrew nodded silently, taking a deep breath. Then he turned and walked unsteadily toward the office. The other three boys felt sick as they watched him go.

"Think he'll crack?" Chad asked.

"Not Andrew," Matt replied, struggling to sound more confident than he felt.

Dean shook his head slowly. "We are so dead."

§

The other boys could hardly pay attention for the next hour during class, fearing at any moment their names would also be called over the intercom. But the dreaded announcement never came. When the bell rang, they hurried out into the hall, desperate for some news.

They looked toward the principal's office just in time to see Andrew step outside, shake Mr. Gibson's hand, and then walk down the hall toward them.

"What the heck happened in there?" Matt asked as Andrew approached.

Andrew waited until he was closer before he responded. "I don't think I've ever been more scared in my life," he began. "It wasn't just Mr. Gibson. Ms. Blunt and Staff Sergeant Romanowski were there too. But almost as soon as I got there, I realized they hadn't called me down to question me. They brought me in as a consultant."

"A what?" Dean asked. "That sounds scarily like the word 'culprit.'"

"A consultant, an expert," Andrew clarified. "They recognized the electronics in the Hijacker are pretty sophisticated, so they wanted my input on whether I thought any of the students at our school were capable of creating such a thing."

"And what'd you tell them?" Chad asked.

"I said it was possible but highly unlikely."

"So, you answered without giving an answer," Matt said. "Perfect!"

Andrew nodded. "That was good advice."

"Wait a second," Dean said. "What if that was just a trick, their way of sizing you up to see if *you* were capable of doing it?"

"I didn't get that feeling at all. It helped that Ms. Blunt vouched for me. She said my dedication to wetlands conservation automatically removed me from the list of suspects."

Chad let out a huge sigh of relief. "I'm so thankful you were running your pH balance experiment."

"Tell me about it," Andrew replied.

"So, we're in the clear," Matt said.

Andrew shook his head. "Not necessarily. They've got a long list of suspects, and they're going to keep calling students in until they find the culprit."

"Great." Dean sagged back against his locker. "So we are dead. They're just going to make it slow . . . and painful."

19

Decoys

For the past few weeks, the boys' time had been consumed with recording the show, editing it, and then sneaking the tape into the marsh. But with the Hijacker seized, the following Saturday morning found them moping around the tree house, the finger of blame having yet to point at them but knowing it was only a matter of time before it did.

Suddenly, Matt leaned forward and pounded the table. "I'm sick of this."

"Tell me about it," Dean said, glancing toward the window. "It's even affecting my flowers. I haven't had the heart to water them lately."

"I did it for you," Andrew said. "I noticed they were starting to wilt."

Dean turned toward him. "Thanks, Andy."

"Maybe we should just confess," Chad suggested. "Get it over with. Like Dean said, maybe they'll go easier on us if we come forward on our own."

"Not after waiting this long," Dean said. "That alone will make them want to throw the book at us."

"Exactly my point," Matt replied. "Whether we confess now or later, it won't matter. So, if we're going to go down no matter what, let's do it on our own terms, not theirs."

"What do you mean?" Chad asked as he and the other boys looked at Matt.

"Think about it," Matt said. "Henrietta's angry about our show, because it interferes with her precious broadcast about her precious marsh, which nobody was listening to anyway. But ever since this all came to light, what's everybody talking about?"

"The marsh," Chad said, a light bulb turning on in his head.

"Exactly. Our radio show has done more to raise the profile of her marsh than anything she or Wetlands Unlimited have ever done. Instead of trying to arrest us, they should be thanking us."

"For once, I agree with you, Matt," Dean said. "I never cared about ducks or marshes or anything like that before this, but now I actually find it kind of interesting."

"Precisely my point. And you're just one person. Think of all the other kids who are suddenly waking up to the fact we have a marsh right on the edge of town. Our show has put that place on the map."

"So, what are you suggesting?" Andrew asked.

Matt leaned forward in his chair. "That we go ahead and broadcast our final episode. Blow this thing wide open."

"But how?" Dean asked. "They've got the Hijacker, and even if Andrew could build another one, there's no way we could get it within a hundred feet of that place. She's patrolling it around the clock."

"I think I have a way around that," Matt said, his eyes gleaming as he turned to Andrew. "But it's going to require some input from our resident 'consultant.'"

§

The following day at noon, all four boys filed into the school's shop class, an impressive facility that housed everything from auto repair to woodworking and metal fabricating. Their shop teacher, Mr. Peesker, had forearms like Popeye and a temper to match if a student talked back or displayed unsafe behavior when working in the shop.

At the moment, Mr. Peesker was observing Ben, who was shaping something on the wood lathe.

"Excuse me, Mr. Peesker?" Matt shouted over the sound of the lathe.

Mr. Peesker stepped away from the machine and raised his safety glasses. "What can I do for you, Matt?"

Matt held up a red book, a volume from his dad's handyman encyclopedia set, and opened it to a page he had bookmarked. "I wondered if you could help us make one of these."

Mr. Peesker looked at the page. "A duck decoy, hey? You planning to do some hunting this fall?"

"Maybe. All this talk about that radio program and the marsh got us thinking about ducks and waterfowl and that sort of thing, and we thought it would be fun to try to make some decoys of our favorite birds."

"Well, you're in luck. My grandfather was an expert at making decoys, and he taught me a thing or two about it. In fact, I still have a few of his decoys kicking around my garage. He used to carve them by hand, which took days, but seeing as we have all these wonderful tools at our disposal," he gestured at the shop, "we can certainly speed up the process."

"Sounds great," Matt replied. "When can we start?"

"Any time you like."

"What about right now?"

Mr. Peesker looked at him in surprise and then glanced at his watch. "I guess we can. But before I let you use any of the power tools, we'll have to go through a safety demonstration. Plus, you'll have to supply your own wood. Ben can tell you what to get. Isn't that right, Ben?"

The boys looked over at Ben, who had just shut down the lathe.

"Hey, Ben, what are you working on?" Matt asked.

Ben held up the piece of wood he had been shaping, which roughly resembled a life-sized cow's foreleg. He gestured to the rest of the cow parts, which were in a partially finished state on a nearby table. "Moo."

Matt grinned. "Why am I not surprised?" He turned back to Mr. Peesker. "Sounds great. Let's get started."

§

For the next several days at noon hour and after school, the boys were hard at work in the shop, cutting and gluing layers of wood together, shaping them on the band saw and the drum sander, and putting the finishing touches on the decoys with chisels and paint. After each of them tried to create a decoy on their own, with mixed results, they decided to break things down into an assembly line, with Matt doing the gluing and initial cutting, Dean roughing out the shape on the band saw, Chad finessing things on the drum sander, and Andrew, who was the most artistic, putting on the finishing touches with the chisel, hand sander, and paint. By the end of the week, they had a vast assortment of decoys to show for their efforts, including a variety of ducks, geese, and all sorts of other waterfowl.

"Pretty impressive, boys," Mr. Peesker said. "Especially considering you had no idea how to do this when you walked in here on Monday."

"Thanks," Matt said, standing back to take in their work. Some of the decoys certainly looked better than others, the boys having gotten better at making them as the week progressed.

"What's this one for?" Mr. Peesker asked, holding up what looked like an eagle.

"That's an osprey," Andrew said. "We're going to put it on our tree house."

"What are you going to do with the rest of them?"

"Probably give them away as gifts," Matt replied.

"Sounds great. Do you boys mind if I get a picture of you all with them?"

"No problem." Matt gestured for the others to gather around. "Come on, guys."

They posed behind the decoys and smiled as Mr. Peesker snapped a photo. "Perfect," he said. "That one's going in the yearbook."

The boys grinned at each other. The fact Mr. Peesker had no idea what they were up to made the moment that much sweeter.

§

"Think we have enough?" Chad asked as they laid out the decoys on the table in the tree house after school.

"I don't know; what do you think?" Matt said, turning to Andrew.

"It should be enough. But we'll have to test them first to find out."

"I don't know, guys," Dean said, lying on his bunk and bouncing a ball off the bunk above him. "Even if Andrew can figure out a way to make this work, there's no way Joyce is going to agree to record another episode."

Matt reached out and snatched the ball on its next bounce. "We're not going to ask her to record another episode."

"Hey!" Dean sat up, hitting his head on the bottom of the upper bunk. "Ouch! What do you mean?" he asked, rubbing his forehead. "You're going to record without her? There's no way I'm playing Maria again." His voice cracked on the word "Maria," as if to prove his point. "And give me back my ball!"

"That's just it," Matt said, reveling in the other boys' quizzical looks as he bounced Dean's ball on the floor. "None of us are going to record the next episode. We're going to do it live."

He threw the ball to Dean, who caught it without even realizing it, a stunned look on his face. "We're going to do what?"

20

"Dear Editor . . ."

"Not on your life!" Joyce said, Matt having just told her his plan to do a live broadcast of the final episode of *It Came . . . from the Grain.* "We could get arrested. *Arrested.* Have you thought of that?"

"Of course, but—"

"That may be no big deal for you, but I'm sixteen. It could go on my record for life."

"But Joyce, we're not going to get arrested. The worst we'd get is a fine."

"Oh, so you're a legal expert now too?"

"No. My point is, there's nothing linking us to the show. And besides, think of our fans."

Indeed, over the past week, a small protest movement had emerged at school among fans of the show. They were calling for Wetlands Unlimited to return the Hijacker to the marsh and allow the final episode to air.

Joyce crossed her arms in defiance. "I don't care about our fans."

"Then do it for me, your brother, and for Chad."

"Yeah," Chad chimed in, having let Matt do the talking up to that point. "And for Andrew. And don't forget Dean."

Joyce glared at him at the mention of Dean's name.

"You're not helping."

"All we're asking you to do is perform one last time," Matt pleaded. "You helped us write the script, remember? It's a brilliant story. Don't you want people to hear how it ends? Even if we do get caught, fine, we'll get in trouble with the police. But we'll be legendary. This is already getting picked up by the provincial news. You want to be a writer when you grow up. Think of how this'll look on your resume!"

"What, a prison sentence?"

"You know what I mean."

They all fell silent for a moment.

"You know how angry they're going to be if we go ahead with this?" Joyce asked, a smile teasing her lips.

"If?" Matt asked hopefully.

"What makes you think Andrew can even pull this off anyway?"

Matt grinned at Chad, who was standing in the doorway to her bedroom. "Let's just say he has all his ducks in a row, so to speak," Chad replied.

"What do you mean?"

"The less you know, the more you can deny," Matt said. "That's our motto."

She glowered at them. "You guys are a regular bunch of criminals."

Matt held up his hands innocently. "We're just trying to have fun, not hurt anyone. And sometimes the only way to have fun is—"

"Okay, spare me your life philosophy. I'll do it. Just this once. But if we get caught . . .."

"We won't get caught," Matt assured her.

"But if we do—"

"We'll make it up to you," Chad said.

"For the rest of our lives," Matt added, jumping to his

feet and heading to the door.

"Wait a second," Joyce said. "How are you going to let people know this show is happening?"

Matt and Chad grinned at each other. "You'll find out tomorrow," they said in unison.

§

The next day, the *Milligan Creek Review* carried the following letter to the editor.

> Dear Editor,
>
> We are the creators of *It Came . . . from the Grain*. No, we're not writing to reveal our names or to turn ourselves in. While some people, particularly Wetlands Unlimited, Henrietta Blunt, and the RCMP, may be upset by our actions, we did not mean to harm Wetlands Unlimited or Ms. Blunt in any way. We highly value everything they are doing to educate people about our local wetlands. We merely recognized an opportunity and took advantage of it. We should have asked permission beforehand, but we all know it's too late for that now. However, before you judge us too harshly, think of what our radio show has done to put the Milligan Creek Heritage Marsh, not to mention the town of Milligan Creek, on the map. All the same, we are very sorry for any grief our actions may have caused.
>
> On that note, we know of one group of people who are very upset. No, they're not angry the program aired. They're disappointed it

ended right before we had a chance to finish our story. Therefore, we would like to make it up to them. At the risk of angering Ms. Blunt, Wetlands Unlimited, Staff Sergeant Romanowski, and any other stakeholders, we would like to announce a special live broadcast of our final show, to take place at the stroke of midnight this Saturday (technically, 12:00 a.m. this Sunday morning) on the Wetlands Unlimited radio station. This will be the final episode of *It Came . . . from the Grain!* It will be aired one time only, so you won't want to miss it.

We realize Ms. Blunt, Wetlands Unlimited, and Staff Sergeant Romanowski may feel compelled to shut us down, but we plead with you to give us this final opportunity to wrap things up. Then we'll go away. Forever.

Sincerely,

The creators of *It Came . . . from the Grain!*

§

"What a load of malarkey!" Henrietta slammed the newspaper down on Romanowski's desk. "*They* put the Milligan Creek Heritage Marsh on the map? Ha! Can you believe the nerve of these people?"

Romanowski skimmed through the letter to the editor and then dismissed it with a wave of his hand. "It's all bluster. We have the device. There's no way they can broadcast anything."

"What if they create another one?"

"Then we'll find it. There's only so many places they

148

can hide it."

"That's true," Henrietta said, pacing back and forth in front of his desk. "But something tells me they've already thought of that."

"You're paranoid, Henrietta. Which is understandable, considering the circumstances."

Henrietta sighed deeply and nodded, still pacing. "We do have a crack squad of volunteers watching over the place, even as we speak. Especially Mrs. Muller. I've never seen such dedication. She's just like her son."

"See what I mean?" Romanowski said. "We've got all our bases covered."

"Not quite." Henrietta snatched up the newspaper. "But I'm about to do just that." She turned and stomped out of his office.

§

The next day, another letter to the editor appeared in the *Milligan Creek Review.*

> Dear Editor,
>
> Prairie pothole wetlands are the heart and the lungs, the very soul of our region. Spanning the southern half of the prairie provinces and extending south of the border into North Dakota, South Dakota, Minnesota, Iowa, and Montana, the prairie pothole region is one of the best waterfowl breeding grounds on the planet, home to hundreds of species, including many at risk of extinction. These wetlands also keep our water clean, control water levels during wet and dry seasons, and contribute to

our overall quality of life in many ways.

At the same time, our wetlands are disappearing at an alarming rate, with some areas of the province having lost up to 70 percent over the last several years. When wetlands disappear, animals aren't the only ones who suffer; so do people. Which is why I have dedicated my life to educating people about this magnificent resource.

Lately, however, our local wetlands have come under attack by a nefarious, underhanded group, the creators of a radio show that I will not dignify by naming here. Although the authorities have yet to catch up to these miscreants, these eco-terrorists, it is only a matter of time before they are brought to justice.

In a final act of defiance, the creators of this show have used this very newspaper to announce the broadcast of their final episode. While I think it is reprehensible for this paper to have printed their letter, giving the terrorists what amounts to free advertising, I would like to use this same platform to print my official four-word response: That'll be the day!

I will stop this show from airing if it's the last thing I do. But I can't do it alone. Therefore, I am calling on you, the good people of Milligan Creek and surrounding area, the very benefactors of our local marsh, to stand with me in a united front against tyranny, terrorism, and the ruthless bullying of our wetlands. This Saturday night at 11:00 p.m., bring flashlights, canoes, hip waders, night-vision goggles, and any other equipment that may help in our effort to prevent this latest attack. (Note: Please leave firearms at home, at the request of Staff Sergeant Romanowski of the RCMP.)

The terrorists may have spoken, but they will not have the last word.

Sincerely,

Henrietta Blunt, Wetlands Unlimited

§

The next day, Matt tossed the newspaper on the table in their tree house. "The gauntlet has been thrown."

Chad scooped it up and scanned Henrietta's letter. "Terrorists? Did she really call us eco-terrorists?"

Dean looked up from watering his flowers. "The show *is* scary."

Matt laughed. "Not nearly as scary as Henrietta Blunt on a rampage. How're those decoys coming along, Andy?"

Andrew looked up from where he was hunched over a decoy of a white-winged scoter, a tendril of smoke curling up from the soldering iron in his hand, the remains of his remote-controlled boat lying in pieces around him. "Pretty good," he said. "I should be ready for a test tonight."

"It better work," Dean said. "Or we're going to look like terrorists *and* tools."

21

HICCUPS

The following Saturday dawned like any other, the sun breaking over the horizon, casting the marsh and the surrounding fields in a golden glow. The sunlight also silhouetted four figures trudging single file, their long shadows stretching across a freshly swathed hayfield, which was dotted with large round bales.

"Why didn't we just ride our bikes?" Dean groaned. "And did we have to do this so early? It's bad enough we have to do the broadcast tonight, but now—"

"Car!" Chad cried.

They ducked behind a round bale.

"That answer your question?" Matt whispered.

Chad peeked around the side of the bale. "It's her!"

The other three boys chanced a glimpse, confirmed it was Henrietta's truck, and then ducked back into hiding.

"Does she always show up this early?" Dean asked.

"We're just lucky she didn't sleep here last night," Matt said. "That's what I heard she's been doing ever since she found the Hijacker. Speaking of which, Andy, how soon until we need to place another decoy?"

Andrew consulted the surveyor's wheel, which he had been pushing along in front of him. It was a device that measured distance as it rolled along the ground. "About a hundred meters."

Chad peeked around the bale again. "She just went inside the interpretive center. Let's go!"

Keeping to a crouch, the boys hurried off, running from bale to bale, Andrew in the lead as he pushed the measuring wheel to record their distance.

§

At breakfast later that morning, Dean could hardly keep his eyes open. Mrs. Muller shook her head and clucked her tongue when she saw him yawn for the umpteenth time. "I don't know about letting him sleep over in that tree house anymore, Dennis," she said to her husband, who was reading the paper as he sipped his coffee. "Just look at him."

"I'm fine, Mom." Dean wiped his bleary eyes. "I just need a shower and a short nap."

"What do you boys do until all hours up there anyway?" Mrs. Muller asked. "And why were your shoes so dirty when you got home? Like you'd been traipsing around in mud. And that smell! I sure hope you aren't getting into any sort of trouble, although if I know Matt Taylor—"

"Just talking, laughing, joking around. You know how it is."

Mrs. Muller looked at her husband for input. His face was still buried in his newspaper. "Dennis?" she said, exasperated.

"What?" He looked up and saw his wife's angry eyes. "Oh, uh, well, I'm sure they get in a bit of mischief now and then, but boys will be boys, right? Just be thankful he's not caught up in this 'It Came from the Grain' fiasco. Looks like there's going to be quite a brouhaha down at

154

the old marsh tonight."

Dean swallowed hard, his scrambled eggs almost getting stuck in his throat on the way down. "Oh yeah?" he said, trying to act casual. "What kind of brouhaha?"

"Oh, come on, Dean," his mother said. "I'm sure you've heard about that silly radio show all the kids are crazy about. Haven't you listened to it?"

Dean shrugged. "A bit."

Mrs. Muller put her hands on her hips. "Are you involved in it somehow?"

Dean swallowed hard, his face reddening. "What do you mean?"

"I saw a note; it fell out of your backpack. It was about a radio show. Little people—and cows."

Dean's pulse slowed in relief. "That was for English class. Once the news broke about the radio show, Mr. Priebe got all excited about us writing our own radio drama in class, but then he got distracted by something else. You know how he is."

Mrs. Muller studied him for a moment and then sniffed. "Well, I, for one, am going to the marsh tonight to show my support for Ms. Blunt and all she's doing to keep our wetlands safe."

Dean looked at her in surprise. "You are?"

"Yes," she replied, drying a pan with a dish towel, the smell of bacon still lingering in the air. "Your father and I both are."

Mr. Muller looked up from his newspaper. "What's this? What am I doing?"

"You're going to the marsh with me tonight to help Ms. Blunt put an end to this radio show nonsense."

"Do I have to?"

Mrs. Muller glared at him.

"I'll take that as a yes." He took a quick sip of coffee

155

and then returned to his paper.

"I think Dean should come with us too," she added.

Dean's eyes went wide, his last forkful of scrambled eggs halfway to his mouth. "What?"

"I'm surprised you're not the one insisting we go with you," Mrs. Muller said, putting some dishes away in the cupboard. "What with your recent interest in the marsh and all."

"I don't know, Mom, I'm pretty tired." Dean stretched and forced a yawn.

"So, have a nap, like you said." She gave the counter a final wipe. "And prepare yourself for another long night."

"But Mom—"

"You heard your mother, Dean." Mr. Muller folded the paper and set it on the table as he stood up. "Besides, I think it'll be fun. We'll make a family event of it, hey, honey?" He went over and gave Mrs. Muller a squeeze.

"Now you're talking," she said, smiling as Dean stared forlornly at his empty plate.

§

"Not so fast," Mrs. Taylor said as Matt and Chad scooped up a piece of toast each and headed for the door.

Matt stopped, the toast halfway to his mouth. "What?"

"Where are you boys going in such a hurry?"

"To the tree house."

"What for?"

"You know, to hang out."

"With who?"

"The guys."

Mrs. Taylor pursed her lips. "You two sure have been spending a lot of time up there lately."

Matt glanced at Chad. "That's why we built it. To spend

time in it."

At that moment, Joyce sauntered into the kitchen and grabbed an orange before heading to the door.

"And where are you going?" Mrs. Taylor asked.

Joyce glanced at her brothers and then back at her mother. "To the tree house. Why?"

Mrs. Taylor's eyebrows lifted in surprise. "You? Go to the tree house? With them?"

"Why not? They are my brothers."

"Yes, but . . . anyway," Mrs. Taylor waved her hand in dismissal, "I'm glad you're all here. I wanted to talk to you about the big event tonight."

"Event?" Matt asked innocently. "What event?"

"At the marsh. I really think we should all go as a family. Show our support."

"No can do." Joyce headed toward the door. "I already have plans."

She was outside before her mother could reply. Mrs. Taylor turned her attention to her sons instead.

"Sorry, Mom." Matt gave Chad a tug. "We'd love to go, but we already promised Andrew we'd help him with a project this evening."

"What kind of project?"

Stumped, Matt paused at the door, looking back at Chad for support.

"A science-y type project," Chad said. "You know Andy." He spun his index finger in circles at his temple. "That mind of his is always working."

"Speaking of which, we need to help him get some stuff ready. See ya, Mom." Matt opened the door and pulled Chad along with him.

As soon as the screen door banged shut, Mr. Taylor entered the kitchen.

"Can you believe it?" Mrs. Taylor asked. "Joyce is

hanging out with her brothers in the tree house."

"Really?" Mr. Taylor helped himself to some coffee. "Well, I can think of worse things she could be doing at her age."

"So can I," Mrs. Taylor said. "But don't you think it's a little strange?"

"On the contrary," he said, wrapping his arms around her, "I think having the house to ourselves on a Saturday morning is excellent."

Mrs. Taylor looked up at him and smiled. "Maybe you're right."

§

On top of the tree house, the osprey decoy looked menacing as it glared down at the forest below, it's wings outstretched, as if ready to dive down and capture its prey.

Inside, Andrew was already setting up the microphones and other recording gear as Joyce sat in one of the bucket seats making notes on the script.

"Where's Dean?" Matt asked as he climbed through the trapdoor.

"Haven't seen him," Andrew said. "Speaking of which, we may have a problem."

"What's the matter now?" Chad asked, right behind his brother.

"Henrietta called my parents last night."

"And?" Matt asked nervously.

"She issued a special invitation—more like a demand—that I be at the showdown tonight. She thinks my dedication to the marsh will inspire other young people across the community to follow my example."

"And?" Joyce said, looking up from her script.

Andrew shrugged. "What could I say?"

"But the broadcast," Matt said. "There's no way we can do it without you."

"Not necessarily," Andrew replied. "Once I've got it all set up, all you have to do is flick this switch," he pointed to a large toggle switch on an amplifier, "and you'll be live to air."

"What if we have some kind of technical problem?" Chad asked.

"Not to mention the sound effects," Joyce added.

"Chad and Matt can handle the sound effects on their own," Andrew said. "As for any technical glitches, we've tested the system, and it works. So, all we can do is cross our fingers. Even if something does go wrong, there's not much we can do from here anyway."

"Can't you just fake sick?" Matt asked.

Andrew shook his head. "For one thing, it would seem a bit too convenient. Plus, then my mom would insist on staying home with me, so I still couldn't be here. Look on the bright side. It may be good to have me on the ground there in case something goes wrong."

"What else could go wrong?" Matt asked as he sank into a chair.

Just then, the trapdoor popped open, and Dean stuck his head through it. "Bad news, guys."

"Let me guess," Matt said. "Henrietta called your house too."

"Worse," Dean replied. Then he did a double take. "Wait a second, who did Henrietta call?"

22

BATTLE STATIONS

Mrs. Muller looked at the thermometer and then felt Dean's forehead. "That's strange. You don't feel very warm, but the thermometer says you're burning up. We'd better check it again." She shook the thermometer to reset it.

Dean rolled onto his side and glanced up at his bedside lamp, which he had just held the thermometer against to heat it up while his mother was out of the room, a trick he had learned from watching the movie *E.T.* "Do we have to? My throat hurts, and I think the thermometer irritates it."

Mrs. Muller sighed. "I guess not. We can't argue with science. You must be terribly disappointed though. The timing couldn't be worse."

Dean cast a worried look over his shoulder. "What do you mean?"

"What with the stand-off at the marsh and all. Maybe your father and I should stay home from it too. I don't like you being here alone if you're not feeling well. What if the government orders another quarantine?"

"What? Mom, that wasn't a real—no, please, don't stay home because of me. I'll be fine. I'm sure it's just from being up late so many nights in the tree house."

"Exactly," Mrs. Muller said, standing up. "But I still think we should all stay home tonight."

Dean rolled toward her. "Henri—Ms. Blunt—is already going to be disappointed I won't be there. She'll be *really* disappointed if you and Dad don't show up either." He lay back on his pillow and grimaced in mock pain. "Do it for Ms. Blunt, Mom. If not for her, do it for the ducks."

Mrs. Muller looked at Dean and smiled fondly. "Look at that, my little Deanie Zucchini is growing up." She reached forward and ruffled his hair. "Don't you worry about those ducks, Dean. You stay in bed and rest. Your father and I will stand with Ms. Blunt and make sure no one interferes with her radio station again."

When she was gone, Dean looked at the digital clock on his bedside table. It was 8:00 p.m. He lay back on his pillow and smiled. Now all he had to do was wait.

§

Three hours later, the marsh, was buzzing with people, vehicles, and equipment. A command center had been set up, complete with a snack table. Staff Sergeant Romanowski directed traffic, while Henrietta supervised a group of men installing floodlights on top of the observation tower.

"This is perfect!" Henrietta said, pacing back and forth behind the men like a general inspecting her troops. She paused and scanned the horizon with her binoculars. "There's no way those little malefactors will be able to sneak in here tonight!"

"Excuse me, Ms. Blunt," one man said as he secured a halogen floodlight onto the railing.

"Call me Henrietta," she replied, lowering her binoculars. "What is it?"

He pointed at the water beneath the tower. "I'm just

162

wondering what kind of bird that is."

Henrietta peered down at it and then smiled. "That, my good man, is a bufflehead."

"Do they normally just sit there like that?" the man asked. "Bobbing in place?"

"Not usually," Henrietta replied. "But—"

"And what about that other one way over there going around and around in a figure-eight pattern?"

"That would be a white-winged scoter, if I'm not mistaken. Probably just curious about all the ruckus." She peered at it through her binoculars. "That is rather odd swimming behavior though. I do hope all this activity isn't interfering with their regular feeding and nesting patterns." She lowered her binoculars. "Well, it's just for one night. Now, if you'll excuse me, gentlemen, I want to see how things are going back at the interpretive center."

As her feet pounded down the stairs, the observation tower shook, causing the head of the decoy owl to wobble slightly. Someone looking closely at it might have noticed a faint glow coming from inside.

When Henrietta arrived at the interpretive center, Andrew was at the base of the tower installing an electronic device bursting with a rainbow of wires as his parents looked on.

"And you must be the Loewens," Henrietta said, shaking their hands. "Great to meet you. You must be so proud of your boy."

"We certainly are," Mr. Loewen replied.

"Though we hardly understand what he's up to half the time," his wife added.

"How's the signal jammer coming along, Andrew?" Henrietta asked.

"Almost finished," Andrew replied as he tightened a screw. It wasn't really a signal jammer; it was just a hand-

163

ful of parts he had thrown together after Henrietta asked him to make one, but she was none the wiser.

Henrietta shook her head in wonder. "Amazing. What are you kids going to come up with next?"

"That's what I'd like to know," a woman's voice said.

Henrietta, Andrew, and the Loewens turned to see who it was. "Mrs. Muller!" Henrietta said. "So good to see you! And this must be your husband." She shook Mr. Muller's hand vigorously.

"Nice to meet you, Ms. Blunt," Mr. Muller said.

"Call me Henrietta, please!" She looked around. "Where's my number one birdwatcher?"

"Dean?" Mrs. Muller asked. "I'm sorry, but it turns out he has a fever. Too many late nights out with his friends, I think." She glared at Andrew, who appeared to be engrossed in his signal-jamming device.

"That's too bad," Henrietta said, turning as she heard someone else approach. "I hate for him to miss out on a moment like this. And who might you fine people be? Here to help us fight the terrorists?"

"I don't know about terrorists," Mrs. Taylor said as she and Mr. Taylor joined the group, "but we're definitely here to support you and the marsh. I'm Anne Taylor, by the way. And this is my husband, Steve. Our boys are Matthew and Chad. I believe they've spent some time out here helping you, along with Dean and Andrew."

"Indeed, they have," Henrietta said, shaking hands with the Taylors. "Fine boys, all of them."

"Speaking of which," Mrs. Taylor continued, "Andrew, I thought Chad and Matt were spending the evening with you, working on some kind of science project."

"Oh, really," Mrs. Muller said, her suspicion rising.

Andrew stared at his device for a moment, scrambling to come up with an explanation. "Uh, they are," he stammered. "They're, uh, they're at a remote signal-jamming station I set up. Just in case this device fails."

"See what I mean?" Henrietta exclaimed. "Kids today are way smarter than we were growing up."

"Some of them, maybe," Mrs. Muller said, not sounding too convinced.

Henrietta clapped her hands and rubbed them together vigorously. "Well, as much as I'd like to stand around chewing the fat, I need to keep moving. Gotta motivate the troops! Feel free to check in at the command center and see what jobs are available," she called back over her shoulder, already walking away. "We've got snacks there too!"

"Thank you!" Mrs. Loewen said.

Mrs. Muller eyed Andrew suspiciously. "Signal jammer, hey?"

Andrew swallowed hard. "Yup."

"Where'd you learn to create something like that?"

"Oh, you know, books."

"Come on, honey, let the man work," Mr. Muller said, putting his arm around his wife's shoulders and pulling her toward the command center. "I think Ms. Blunt said something about snacks."

§

At the entrance to the marsh, Staff Sergeant Romanowski ushered a vehicle inside and then closed the gate behind it. He looked up as Henrietta approached. "How are things going in there?"

"Fabulous!" She checked her watch. "It's nearly time."

"Well, that ought to be the last of them," he said, locking the gate. "I'll post a couple of people here on watch and to unlock the gate in case of emergency. But we have the ambulance on site, so we should be okay."

"The press is here too," Henrietta said. "I just finished doing a radio interview and an interview with the Milligan Creek Review. I hate to admit it, but those terrorists were right about one thing. This uproar is certainly drawing a lot of attention to the marsh."

Romanowski shrugged. "Like they say, there's no such thing as bad press."

Henrietta's eyes narrowed. "Unless it hurts our wetlands."

"Right, of course." Romanowski pushed back his policeman's cap and smoothed his mustache with his thumb and forefinger, as if working up the nerve to say something. "You know, Henrietta, when all this is over—"

"Ms. Blunt!" a woman said, running up behind them, slightly out of breath. "I think everything's in place. Do you want to give any final directions?"

"Just a moment," Henrietta said, turning back to the blushing staff sergeant. "You were saying?"

"Don't worry about it," he replied. "Sounds like they need you back there. We can talk later."

Henrietta raised her fist in defiance. "Stand strong!"

Romanowski raised his fist in reply. "I will."

She turned away from him and raised her megaphone. "Okay, people, battle stations!"

As he watched her jog back to the command center, Romanowski took off his hat, smoothed his thinning hair, and shook his head in wonder. "They sure don't make women like her every day."

"Moo!"

Romanowski spun around, startled. He couldn't see anything in the darkness, his eyes momentarily blinded from looking toward the brightness of the command center. He flicked on his police-issue Maglite and was startled to find himself face-to-face with a cow. Only it didn't look—or sound—like any cow he'd ever seen. In fact, it appeared to be made of wood.

"Moo," it said again, sounding as if the noise had been recorded. Romanowski swung his flashlight to the left and spotted Ben standing beside the cow, startling the staff sergeant once again.

"Good evening, son, what—"

"Can my cow and I come inside?"

Romanowski shifted his flashlight back and forth between the boy and his beast. "You want to bring a cow into the marsh?"

"Yes."

"Why?"

In response, Ben reached behind the cow's ear and flicked a switch. Bright lights shone from the cow's eyes, nearly blinding Romanowski, who raised his hands to shield himself from the powerful beams.

"If they're not going to put a cow in the radio show, I'm going to put a cow in the marsh," Ben said, "and help bust them."

"Be my guest," Romanowski replied, opening the gate. He stood back and watched as Ben trundled through, pulling his cow, which was mounted on a wagon, behind him. Romanowski shook his head in wonder once again. "It takes all kinds."

23

LIVE TO AIR

Despite the dozens of people staked out on the observation tower and around the interpretive center, gliding through the marsh in canoes, stationed along the wooden walkway, hunkered down in duck blinds, and scanning the water with floodlights, all was silent, save for the sound of a male bobolink being broadcast through a set of loudspeakers mounted on the roof of Henrietta's truck.

"There you have it, folks," Henrietta's voice blared over the loudspeakers, part of her recorded show. "Once you can tell the male bobolink from the female, you'll know you're well on your way to becoming—"

"All right, people," Henrietta said over her megaphone, turning down the broadcast for a moment. "It's almost midnight. Everyone count down with me. Ten, nine, eight . . .."

§

"Seven, six, five, four, three . . .." Chad mouthed the final two numbers and then hit "play" on a tape deck that began playing spooky music in the background. Then he pointed to Matt, who nodded and then looked at his script.

"Ladies and gentlemen," Matt began, "humankind is an intelligent species, a powerful species, an innovative and inventive species, able to plumb the ocean's depths and scan the far reaches of space."

§

Out at the marsh, everyone stared at the loudspeakers in stunned silence as Matt's voice, disguised by Andrew's pitch modulator, boomed over the bulrushes. "But human beings are also proud creatures, prone to think too highly of themselves, to believe they are capable of anything. But wherever the light of human knowledge shines, it can't help but create shadows, murky pockets of ignorance, mystery, and fear."

"They're here!" Henrietta shouted through her megaphone, jumping on top of the truck roof. "Everybody, red alert! I repeat, red alert!"

§

"Chester!" Maria, cried. "Hurry! They're coming! They're coming!"

"Wait, I forgot to close the machine shed doors," Chester, replied. "Here, take the sledgehammer, and head down to the basement. I'll be right there."

"But Chester—"

"Just go!"

Chad and Matt ran in place in wooden boxes full of grass to simulate the sound of the couple running across the farmyard. Then Matt pointed at Dean.

"These doors," Chester said, his voice straining with exertion. "They're stuck."

Chad hit "play" on a tape deck that played the sound of farm machinery starting up.

"Oh no!" Chester said as the machines continued to roar, getting closer. "I'll never be able to—wait, that's it! The roof!"

§

At the marsh, people yelled directions to each other, beams of light swept across the flooded landscape, and canoe paddles turned the water to froth as the searchers scoured the area for any sign of the interlopers.

"I see them!" someone shouted. "Over there!"

A dozen lights converged on the spot, revealing nothing more than an old fencepost with a tuft of grass stuck on top.

"False alarm!"

"Keep looking!" Henrietta ordered as the radio show continued to air.

§

"There, I made it," Chester said. "I'm safe for the moment. But now what?"

Chad cranked the volume on the machinery sounds.

"Oh no! The farm machinery has surrounded the farmhouse! They're going to try to knock it down! I have to find a way to get Maria out of there. Unless . . .."

§

Out at the marsh, the initial burst of activity was slowing down, more and more people stopping and listening to the broadcast rather than continuing the search.

"Come on, people!" Henrietta shouted over the megaphone. "Don't stop now! We almost have them!"

Near the interpretive center, Andrew looked around nervously, glancing up at the owl decoy at the top of the radio tower.

"Signal jammer, hey?" Mrs. Muller said, coming up behind him. "Doesn't look like it's doing a very good job, does it?"

Andrew turned toward her, his face white. "Well, like I said, uh, these things are . . . complicated."

"Or maybe they're really something else!" Mrs. Muller pounced on the device and pulled the plug, holding it up in triumph. The radio show continued uninterrupted.

"I told you the boys had nothing to do with this," Mr. Muller said, coming up behind her and taking the plug out of her hand.

She stared at the cord in confusion. "But I thought—"

"Let's go get another cup of hot chocolate and listen to the rest of the show," Mr. Muller said, putting his arm around her. "It's actually quite good."

As Andrew watched Mr. Muller lead his stunned wife away, he wiped beads of sweat from his forehead.

§

"Good thing the old owners left a pile of scrap metal beside the machine shed," Chester said. "These old bike handlebars are perfect. The rubber handles should protect me from getting electrocuted, and the power lines will make a perfect zip line, taking me straight from the machine shop to the house."

A crash sounded in the background.

"Oh no! The machines are ramming the house. I just hope I'm not too late. Okay, here goes nothing. Three, two, one."

§

Even Henrietta stood in riveted fascination as what sounded like the whiz of fishing line being pulled from a reel echoed across the marsh.

"It's working!" Chester exclaimed. "Hold on, Maria! I'm almost there!"

Suddenly, Henrietta snapped out of it. "That's it. There's only one way to stop these reprobates."

She leaped down from her truck and stomped toward the interpretive center, pushing through a crowd of idle searchers.

Just as she was about to open the door, Staff Sergeant Romanowski intercepted her. "What are you doing?"

"The only thing I can do. I'm pulling the plug on the broadcast board. Shutting the entire thing down."

Henrietta pushed past him and reached for the door handle, but Romanowski put his hand on hers.

"Wait."

She glared at him in anger. "What are you—"

"Look at them."

"Who?"

"Them." He turned her toward the crowd of people, who were standing around like zombies listening to the show. Young people, old people, men and women, all of them completely absorbed. Even the reporter from the radio station had his mic in the air, trying to pick up what he could of the program.

"All these people . . . in your marsh."

"It's not my marsh, it's—"

"I know, the marsh belongs to everyone. The point is, they're here. They're here to show they care. About you and about the wetlands. This is a night none of them will ever forget. Do you really want to pull the plug on that?"

"But the terrorists! We have to—"

"They're not terrorists. They're just some kids putting their energy into some harmless, creative fun."

"But my radio station—"

"Will go back to its regular programming as soon as the show ends. You read what they wrote in the paper. They just want to finish what they started."

Henrietta looked at Romanowski and then down at his hand, which still held hers.

§

"Maria, where are you?" Chester cried as he ran through the house, the possessed machinery roaring and clanking outside.

"I'm down here!" Maria yelled. "In the basement!"

Feet pounded as Chester raced down the stairs.

Clank. Clank.

"It's not working!" Maria cried. "I'm not strong enough."

"Here, give me sledgehammer," Chester said.

Clank. Clank. Clank.

"I think I see a crack!" Maria cried.

Crash!

"Hurry! It sounds like the entire house is going to come down on top of us!"

Clank. Clank. Clunk.

"There! A piece of the wall broke away. Keep swinging! Harder!"

Clunk. Clunk. Crash.

"There, that's big enough," Chester said. "I'll help you through. Then I'll come right behind you."

"Don't forget the journal!" Maria said.

"Here, take it! Now if I can just fit through . . . Ugh.

174

I'm stuck!"

"I'll pull you!" Maria said.

Crash!

"Chester, the entire house, it's—"

Boom!

§

As they stood side by side listening to the broadcast, Staff Sergeant Romanowski released Henrietta's hand and slipped his arm around her shoulders. She looked at his arm in surprise and then slowly turned to face him as the show continued to air.

§

Maria coughed and choked. "Aagh, so much dust. Chester, are you—"

"I'm okay. Here, let me help you up. Looks like we're safe—for the moment."

"Yes, but where are we?"

"In the tunnels, I guess," Chester said. "Just like the map shows."

"But where do they lead?"

"That's what we're about to find out."

Just then, they heard a strange sound from somewhere down the tunnel.

"What's that?" Chester asked. "It sounds like a—"

Moo.

"A cow? Down here? But—"

"Chester, wait. Before you take one more step."

"Maria, this is no time for—"

"I don't know what's going to happen from here on out or what we're going to discover, but I'm sure of one thing: I'm never going to let you out of my arms again. Now come here, you big lug."

§

Up in the tree house, Chad flicked the switch for the tape labeled "kissing sound effect," but nothing happened. He flicked it again, and it snapped right off! In silent panic, he turned to the others, switch in hand.

Not missing a beat, Dean crossed the tree house and grabbed Joyce in his arms. "Don't worry, Maria," he said into Joyce's mic as she struggled to break free. "There's no place I'd rather be." Then he leaned in close . . . and kissed her.

Joyce's eyes went wide with shock—and anger.

§

At precisely the same moment, Staff Sergeant Romanowski pulled back from kissing Henrietta. She wiggled her nose. "Your mustache. It tickles."

Romanowski rubbed his upper lip self-consciously. "I can shave it off, if you like."

She squeezed his chin playfully. "Not on your life."

The crowd burst into applause as ominous music played over the loudspeakers. Henrietta looked around in surprise and then started to clap, thinking they were applauding the end of the radio program. Then she realized everyone was smiling at her and the staff sergeant.

"Take a bow, Henrietta," Romanowski said, smiling as he took off his policeman's cap and did exactly that. "Take a bow."

24

BACK TO NATURE

"We did it!" Dean said, pulling off his headphones. "I just wish Andrew was here to celebrate with us." Then he noticed Joyce glaring at him. "Um, I'm sorry, Joyce. The sound effect wasn't working, and I—"

"Don't worry about it," she said, taking off her headphones and running her fingers through her hair. "You saved the show. And it was kind of . . . sweet."

Dean's eyebrows shot to the top of his forehead. "Really? You mean you're not—"

Joyce scowled at him. "Don't get any ideas. It was strictly business."

"Of course." Dean cleared his throat and lowered his voice. "Strictly business."

Matt and Chad could barely contain their laughter.

Suddenly, Dean looked at his watch. "Uh oh, I'd better go. Gotta get home before Mom and Dad, or I'm a dead duck. See ya!"

"See ya," Matt said as Dean flipped open the trapdoor. "You did a great job, by the way. You made a way better Chester than I would have done."

"Thanks!" Dean said.

"Not to mention the fact you saved me from having

to kiss my sister." Matt flinched as Joyce smacked him on the arm.

"Just don't let it go to your head, dream boy!" Chad said as Dean sped down the ladder, his face glowing with elation.

§

At school on Monday, all everyone could talk about was the "showdown at the marsh," as it was being called.

Standing by their lockers, the boys basked in the afterglow of the experience. It was all they could do to keep silent about their involvement in the caper.

"I'm glad we got to air our last show, but it's too bad we had to leave the audience with more questions than answers," Dean said.

"Maybe we can do a sequel," Chad suggested. "Like Matt said."

"Forget it," Dean replied. "We got lucky. This time."

"It's always better to leave them wanting more anyway," Matt added.

He looked up just as Ben entered the hallway. Matt's eyes widened with surprise when he saw him. Instead of his typical bedhead, for perhaps the first time in recorded memory, Ben's hair was combed and styled neatly, completely transforming his appearance.

"Is that . . . mousse in his hair?" Chad whispered.

"More like *moo*-ouse," Dean quipped. The other boys giggled as Ben approached.

"Hey, Ben, how was your weekend?" Matt asked. "Did you catch the final episode of that radio show?"

"Yep."

"And?"

Ben grinned. "It was *moo-st* enjoyable."

The other boys broke into laughter as Ben walked off with a huge grin on his face.

"Well, it's been a blast, guys," Matt said, putting his arm around Andrew's shoulders. "And we owe it all to our resident genius here. Creating a bunch of mini-hijackers, hiding them in the decoys, and using them to leap-frog the signal from one bird to the next all the way from the tree house to the marsh was brilliant."

Andrew smiled. "Thanks, but it was your idea. I just figured out a way to pull it off. And if Dean hadn't of come up with that woodpecker story, Henrietta never would have installed the owls, which made perfect hiding spots for the last two hijackers. I just wish we had been able to grab our decoys yesterday. I don't want Henrietta getting her hands on them, never mind the police."

"Don't worry about it," Matt said. "We can pick them all up tonight. Besides, we did such a good job of making them, no one will ever be able to tell the difference between the decoys and the real thing."

Andrew didn't look nearly as confident. "I hope not."

§

Out at the marsh, Henrietta and a handful of volunteers, including Mrs. Muller, were picking up garbage, dismantling equipment, and otherwise restoring the marsh to its normal state. "I don't know if this place will ever be the same," Henrietta said, pausing on the wooden walkway and looking out at the glistening water.

"I don't think any of us will be either," Mrs. Muller replied, rubbing her aching back. Like Dean, she hadn't exactly volunteered to help, but she had felt too guilty to refuse when Henrietta asked.

"I hope not," Staff Sergeant Romanowski said, coming

up beside the two women.

Henrietta smiled in surprise. "Richard! What are you doing out here?"

Mrs. Muller seized the moment to slip away to her car.

"Oh, just thought I'd stop by to see how the clean-up is going."

"Great," Henrietta said. "In fact, I was just thinking about writing another letter to the editor."

"Oh yeah? To thank the volunteers?"

"Yes, that and to make a proposal."

Romanowski eyed her expectantly. "A proposal?"

"Yes. This may sound crazy, but I was wondering about inviting the creators of 'It Came from the Grain' to make their broadcast an annual event. Only maybe their next series could be set in the marsh." She looked at Romanowski and smiled. "And feature a dashing young police officer as the hero."

Romanowski grinned, his mustache bristling. "I guess you could say the possibilities are . . . unlimited!"

They smiled lovingly at each other and then turned and stared out at the water.

"Hey, what's that?" Romanowski asked a moment later, pointing.

Henrietta squinted until she spotted a white-winged scoter swimming in a figure-eight pattern out in the open water. "That's strange. It was doing the same thing on Saturday night. I wonder if I should try to catch it, put it under observation."

Just then, the bird slowed and then stopped, drifting in the still water before disappearing into the bulrushes.

"I don't know." Romanowski turned and smiled at Henrietta. "Maybe we should just let nature take its course."

In what was becoming a habit every time she was in the handsome staff sergeant's presence, Henrietta blushed.

A Brief Note on
It Came . . . from the Grain

I've been a big fan of "old time radio" for some time, radio programs from the 1930s to the 1960s featuring stories of suspense and intrigue. So, when it came to figuring out what the boys were going to broadcast, a radio play seemed the natural choice.

I came up with the title, *It Came . . . from the Grain*, while driving across Saskatchewan doing writing workshops at various schools. I thought it was a fun title, and I had some ideas for what it might be about, but I decided to develop the idea with students over the next few weeks to see what they came up with.

To say I was blown away by the students' creativity would be an enormous understatement. I've actually considered writing a collection of short stories based on the ideas we developed together. They were that good! In fact, some of the pitches the boys make in the book come from those very workshops (although Dean's suggestion of the little people who hatch when the grain is planted and then disappear at the end of the season was my original idea).

The story about the haunted farm machinery that I wound up using in the book came from the first workshop I did on the topic in Craik, SK. The buried community was inspired by a trip to my father-in-law's birthplace, Vantage, SK, which is now nothing but an empty field with a stone marker indicating where the community once stood.

I would like to thank all the students and teachers who participated in those brainstorming exercises, and I hope they get a kick out of knowing they played a role in the creation of this book.

UP THE CREEK!

When Matt, Chad, Dean, and Andrew set out on a canoe trip down Milligan Creek during spring runoff season, little do they realize their voyage through small-town Saskatchewan is about to turn into one of the wildest experiences of their lives—if they survive!

THE WATER WAR

When a beautiful new girl moves to Milligan Creek, everyone in town is so smitten that her mere presence threatens to ruin the perfect summer that Matt has planned for him, his brother, Chad, and their best friends, Andrew and Dean. So, the boys come up with what seems like the perfect distraction: a water war. It's the ultimate game of survival, where every player is both hunter and prey. But when the new girl decides to join in, the game that was supposed to unite the boys against the interloper threatens to tear their close friendship apart.

THE GREAT GRAIN ELEVATOR INCIDENT

When Milligan Creek's iconic grain elevators are slated for demolition, to be replaced by a huge, ugly inland grain terminal a couple of miles from town, Matt, Chad, Andrew, and Dean concoct a wild scheme to save their grain elevators—and their small prairie community—from being wiped off the face of the planet.

Snowbound!

When a number of mysterious snow tunnels begin to show up in the ditches around the small town of Milligan Creek, Matt and Chad Taylor and their best friends, Dean and Andrew ,are determined to figure out who is making them and why. As they hunt for the person responsible, the mysterious tunnels and that winter's record snowfall inspires them to create their own epic snow maze, to which they plan to charge admission. However, with a once-in-a-century blizzard forecast to hit the prairies, the race is on to solve the mystery and complete their maze before the entire province is covered in a glistening blanket of white.

For more details, visit www.kevinmillerxi.com.

About the Author

Kevin Miller grew up on a farm outside of Foam Lake, Saskatchewan, where he dreamed of becoming a writer. He got his first break as a newspaper reporter in Meadow Lake, SK. Within a year, he parlayed that into a job in book publishing, which eventually enabled him to become a full-time freelance writer and editor.

From there, Kevin transitioned into film, and he spent the next thirteen years traveling the world while working on a variety of feature films, documentaries, and short film projects. In addition to serving as a writer, he has also worked as a director, producer, and film editor.

These days, Kevin splits his time between filmmaking, writing, editing, and teaching. When he's not working, he enjoys hanging out with his wife and four kids, fishing, hiking, canoeing, skiing, skateboarding, and otherwise exploring his world.

Kevin likes to talk about books, movies, and writing almost as much as he enjoys writing. If you'd like to contact Kevin about any of these topics, to tell him what you think of this novel, or to book him for a speaking engagement, you can reach him at www.kevinmillerxi.com.